BORNE ALOFT BY A FIERCE LIONBIRD!

You are awakened from a restless sleep by the frantic whinnying of your horse. Raising your head, you see a huge black shadow hovering in the gray light of dawn above your tethered mount. The fearsome creatures has the hindquarters of a lion and the head of a giant bird, and you recognize it instantly as a griffon!

Drawing your gleaming sword, Fireborn, you rush to your horse's aid, only to have the fearsome winged monster turn on you instead!

You're helpless in the grasp of the lionbird as it pulls your struggling body closer. Its huge wings fan the cold mountain air around you, and you feel the beast lift you as easily as a mother might lift her new baby and soar upward into the dawn sky.

What will you do?

If you decide to attack the griffon, roll two dice to hit and add your fighting skill score to the result. If the total is 12 or more, turn to **48.** If the total is less than 12, subtract 5 hit points of damage from your total hit points and turn to **65.**

Whatever you decide, only your decisions, and the luck of the dice roll, can hope to rescue the
PRISONERS OF PAX THARKAS

A **SUPER ENDLESS QUEST**™
Adventure Gamebook #1

PRISONERS
of
PAX THARKAS

BY MORRIS SIMON

Cover Art by Keith Parkinson
Interior Art by Mark Nelson

TSR, Inc.
PRODUCTS OF YOUR IMAGINATION™

To "Mom" with love: thank you

Distributed to the book trade in the United States by Random House, Inc., and in Canada by Random House of Canada, Ltd.
Distributed in the United Kingdom by TSR UK, Ltd.
Distributed to the toy and hobby trade by regional distributors.

DUNGEONS & DRAGONS, ADVANCED DUNGEONS & DRAGONS, and AD&D are registered trademarks owned by TSR, Inc.

SUPER ENDLESS QUEST, DRAGONLANCE, PRODUCTS OF YOUR IMAGINATION, and the TSR logo are trademarks owned by TSR, Inc.

First printing: February, 1985
Printed in the United States of America
Library of Congress Catalog Card Number: 84-91364
ISBN: 0-88038-209-0

9 8 7 6 5 4 3 2 1

TSR, Inc.
P.O. Box 756
Lake Geneva, WI 53147

TSR UK Ltd.
The Mill, Rathmore Road
Cambridge CB1 4AD
United Kingdom

AN EXCITING NEW EXPERIENCE IN BOOKS!

Welcome, you who are about to become a prisoner of Pax Tharkas, to an exciting, totally new concept in role-playing gamebooks.

Based on the popular DUNGEONS & DRAGONS® and ADVANCED DUNGEONS & DRAGONS® games, SUPER ENDLESS QUEST™ Adventure Gamebooks require only two standard six-sided dice, an ample supply of luck—and, most of all, your skill in making decisions as you play the game. If dice are unavailable, a simple alternative, requiring only pencil and paper, may be used instead.

SUPER ENDLESS QUEST™ Adventure Gamebooks have been designed to read easily, without complicated rules to slow down the story. Once you have read through the simple rules that follow, you should seldom find it necessary to refer back to them. Your options are repeated clearly in the text at each choice point, with occasional reminders about additional options you may wish to consider to improve your chances. Your adventure reads like a book, plays like a game, and offers a thrill a minute—with YOU as the hero!

YOUR CHARACTER

In this book, you are Bern Vallenshield, a young Ranger of twenty whose home is in the Crystalmir valley region of the continent of Ansalon in the world of Krynn, described in AD&D® DRAGONLANCE™ adventure game modules and the novel trilogy, DRAGONLANCE™ CHRONICLES.

Your world is an unusual one, inhabited by elves, dwarves, and other, often dangerous, creatures, but so far it has been a reasonably good one.

Armed with your mighty volcanic steel sword Fireborn, given to you by your father, you have honed your Ranger skills during many adventures in the dangerous forests of Crystalmir valley. You don't know it yet, but you are about to face your greatest challenge, in the form of the evil Dragon Highlord Verminaard and his legions of magical fire-breathing dragons and other fearsome creatures that threaten your homeland. . . .

PLAYING THE GAME

ESTABLISHING YOUR CHARACTER

YOUR Bern will be different from someone else's because YOU help to create him.

Carefully tear out the removable **Character Stats Card** you will find at the beginning of this book. This card is your record of Bern's character makeup. It also doubles as a bookmark if you should need to mark your place to refer back to the rules.

Since we hope you will be playing this adventure many times, it is suggested that you write on the card in pencil only, so that your character stats can be erased easily when you are ready to play again. If you have access to a photocopier, you may wish to make several photocopies of the Character Stats Card before you fill it in. Another alternative is to reproduce the card by writing on a 3″ × 5″ card or a slip of paper.

You are now ready to round out Bern's individual identity by establishing his strengths and weaknesses. Your character's **name** (Bern Vallenshield), **age** (20), and **character class** (Ranger) have already been entered for you. Before you fill out the rest of the card, it is necessary for you to understand the game's scoring system.

SCORING

Playing the game requires you to keep track of three things—**hit points, skill points**, and **experience points**—on the tear-out **Character Stats Card** located at the front of the book. An explanation of each of these follows.

HIT POINTS

You, as Bern, have a specific life strength, represented by **hit points**. Once hit points are reduced to zero, Bern Vallenshield ceases to exist, and you have come to the end of your adventure, whether the text has come to an end or not.

You lose hit points each time you fail, through the roll of the dice, to hit your enemy, because your opponent succeeds in hitting you back. As a result, you must deduct a stated number of hit points from your hit point total.

You may also lose hit points through sneak attacks or perhaps through carelessness when you have no chance to fight back. In such instances, roll one die for **damage**. The result of the die roll is deducted from your total points.

Bern Vallenshield, as a reasonably experienced Ranger, starts out the adventure with 30 hit points, plus one random chance to improve this score. Roll one six-sided die and add the total to 30 for your total hit points. Record this number in the blank space labeled "hit points." If you roll 1, 2, 3, or 4 and are dissatisfied with the result, you have one additional chance to improve it. You may, if you wish, roll again, but you *must* accept the result of the second die roll, even if it is smaller than your first roll. During the course of the game, do not erase the original number of hit points, since you may need to refer to it at certain times when your character is "healed."

Guard Bern's hit points carefully, but don't be afraid to spend them when the goal seems worthwhile. At various times throughout the adventure, you will have the opportunity to recover some of your hit points by means of a **healing throw**. However, it is important to remember that *you can never recover more hit points than you had at the start of your adventure.*

SKILL POINTS

Now you are ready to determine your character's **skills**.

Skill points allow you to increase your chances of success by adding Bern's score for a specific skill to the dice roll. In this book, you will be asked to divide 9 skill points in any way you want, provided that you give Bern at least one point in each of his three skills.

Bern Vallenshield's skills in this book are **fighting, observation**, and **physical prowess**.

Fighting

Your **fighting** skill score increases your chance of success in combat.

When you fight an opponent in this book, roll two dice and add the sum of the dice to your fighting skill score. If the result is equal to, or larger than, the number required to "hit" (given in the text), you are successful.

Observation

Your **observation** skill score increases your ability to observe, such as in finding secret doors, or to avoid being observed, such as in trying to sneak past an enemy.

To use your observation skill, roll one die and add the result to your observation skill score. If the total is equal to, or greater than, the number given in the text, you have succeeded.

Physical Prowess

Your **physical prowess** score increases your chances of success in feats involving physical strength or speed, such as in trying to break down a door or in fleeing from a pursuing enemy.

To use your physical prowess skill, roll one die and add the result to your physical prowess skill score. If the total equals or exceeds the number given in the text, you are successful.

Unlike hit points, which may decrease or increase during the adventure, skill points remain constant throughout the game. However, as you play and replay the adventure, you will want to experiment with different combinations of skill points to determine what works best.

You have 9 total skill points, which you may divide in any way you wish between Bern Vallenshield's skill categories—**fighting, observation**, and **physical prowess**. The only exception is that you must place at least 1 skill point in each skill category. Now fill in the blanks for your three skills on the Character Stats Card. Remember, your placement of skill points can have a great effect on the outcome of your adventure, so choose wisely!

EXPERIENCE POINTS

As in real life, experience increases your chances of success in a given situation because you have encountered a similar situation before and understand the various possibilities that may occur. You, as Bern Vallenshield, will begin this adventure with between 1 and 6 **experience points**, depending on the luck of your roll of the dice. You may spend them to increase your chances on *any* dice roll throughout the book, but once experience points are used up, they are gone and they must be deducted from your total.

To use experience points, you must decide how many points you will spend *before* you roll the dice, then add that score to the result of your dice roll. Whether the roll of the dice is successful or not, the experience points are gone and must be deducted from your total.

To determine Bern's **experience points**, roll one six-sided die and record the result in the blank space marked "experience points." If you roll a 1 through 4, you have one, and only one, chance to improve your score by rolling a second time if you wish, but you *must* accept the second roll, even if it is smaller than the first. Remember, your experience points can be used on any dice roll to improve your chances, but once spent, they are used up and must be subtracted from your total experience points.

Use your experience points wisely, saving them for what you consider to be crucial situations. At a number of story endings, you may be rewarded with extra experience points for playing the adventure well.

These bonus points may be added to your total experience points the next time you are ready to play the adventure.

COMBAT

Combat occurs when you choose, or are forced, to fight an enemy—a monster, a person, a ghost. To engage in combat, roll two dice, add them together, and add Bern's fighting skill score to the result of the dice roll. The text will tell you how many points you need to hit the monster. The tougher the enemy, the more points you need to hit it. If the total is sufficient to hit the monster, turn to the "win" section. (Note that the numbered sections you are directed to turn to are section numbers, *not* page numbers.) If you miss, the enemy automatically hits you back, and you will be told how many hit points of damage to deduct from your score. You can turn to the "lose" section immediately, or you can choose to try to strike your enemy again, provided you have not "died" by having your hit point total reduced to zero by your enemy's blow.

This combat sequence may be repeated as many times as you wish (and remain alive), until either you win, you decide you've taken enough damage and turn to the "lose" section, or you are killed by having your hit points reduced to zero.

Some opponents are easier to hit than others, but at the same time, some impose more damage than others, just as in real life. For example, a carrion crawler, with its many tentacles, is quite difficult to hit, but it doesn't inflict as much damage per round as the more easily hit wight, which drains the very life-force from your body when it strikes!

Many combat sections offer **flee** or **surrender** options. You may choose one or the other of these options at any point in combat, as long as Bern Vallenshield is still alive. Obviously you are not going to choose to flee or surrender if you win the combat. But if you lose the first round, you might then consider fleeing or surrendering, after deducting the appropriate number of hit points, rather than turning to the "lose" section.

In some combat segments, however, you must have a certain number of hit points in order to be strong enough to try to flee. Thus you may be strong enough to flee at the start of combat, but after one or more unsuccessful rounds, your character may be too weak to flee and may not exercise this option.

PLAYING WITHOUT DICE

Should you ever wish to play the adventure when dice are unavailable, there is a simple substitute that requires only pencil and paper. Simply write the numbers 1 through 6 on separate slips of paper and mix them up in a container. Then draw one of the slips, note the number, and place it back in the container. Mix up the numbers and draw a second time. Each draw represents one roll of the die. If only one die is called for, draw only one number.

Your character—Bern Vallenshield—is now complete, and you are ready to begin your adventure. Turn to page 15—and good luck!

1

The familiar odor of burning wood as you approach Solace makes your empty stomach rumble as your mind conjures images of Otik, the cook's, specialty at the Inn of the Last Home—spicy, fried potatoes. You've traveled most of the night on the rugged mountain trail, and your home village is only a few miles farther. As tired as you are, your pace quickens as you climb the steep cliff road, eager to see your familiar homeland.

You top the rise, expecting to see the lights of Solace twinkling in the trees. Solace is a tree village. Every dwelling and business in town, with the exception of Theros Ironfeld's blacksmith shop, is built high in the branches of the mighty vallenwood trees. The people of Solace took to the trees during the reign of terror following the terrible Cataclysm, and there they have stayed. Networks of bridges connect Solace, stretching through the leafy bowers just like the limbs of the trees themselves.

But as you reach the crest of the hill, you catch your breath in horror. Something is terribly wrong! Instead of the fragrant, white smoke of home fires drifting up among the leaves, you see a thick pall of greasy black smoke hanging over the valley. You realize that some great catastrophe has come to Solace in your absence! Turn to **93**.

2

"We've got to try to get out of here the quickest way we can," you tell the others. "We know enough about Verminaard's plans to warn everyone in the province who hasn't already been attacked by his dragons. Help me break through these doors!"

You test the heavy panels and find that they're a little loose. The three of you push as hard as you can, trying to force the rusted hinges and brackets off the exterior wall.

Roll one die to see if you are successful in your efforts to force the doors open. Add your physical prowess score to the die roll. If the result is 8 or more, the doors give way. Turn to **15**. If it is less than 8, your efforts to open the doors are unsuccessful. Turn to **76**.

3

Fear seems to add wings to your feet. You can feel the blood pounding in your head, and your breath comes in painful gasps as you tear frantically for your horse.

Suddenly you hear one of the men shout, "Bern, watch out behind you!" Turn to **107**.

4

A feeling of terrible fear sweeps over the group, affecting everyone but the kender. Essa shivers.

"What's in there?" you ask nervously.

"I don't know," she whispers. "But I sense evil in there—as well as good."

"M-Maybe we shouldn't g-g-go in," Kegan says, his voice quavering.

"The guards are bound to get tired of banging on that door pretty soon," Willow says, shrugging. "Maybe they'll leave and we can go try to get the gully dwarves to help us."

"Well, I'm going in, whether you do or not!" Essa says firmly. "There's no way I'm going to hide among a bunch of gully dwarves!"

If you decide to risk entering the Sla-Mori, turn to **115**. If you decide it would be too dangerous to enter the Sla-Mori and instead wait until the guards leave, then seek out the gully dwarves, turn to **35**.

5

You see the kender's hoopak, already poised to deliver its deadly bulletlike stone at the first dragonman to open the door. You grab Kegan's hand and race along the wide corridor connecting the two wings of the citadel. Behind you, a hissing shriek tells you that Willow's sling has found its mark.

The kender is standing in the center of the cavernous hallway, swinging her bullet sling with lightning speed. Its powerful missiles rain against the vallenwood panel as the draconians slam the door closed against her barrage of stones.

"That's enough, Willow!" you shout to the fearless kender girl. "Hurry! We've got to find a place to hide!"

The kender hurls one last stone, denting the heavy

17

wooden door. Then she dashes to join you at the other end of the corridor. Inside the carpeted hallway, you nod toward the stairs to the cellar. "If we can get down there before they see where we've gone, we might have a chance to hide until it's dark enough to sneak out of the fortress!" Turn to **131**.

6

It's almost completely dark by the time the caravan stops on the outskirts of Gateway. The goblin guards and their draconian overseers set the women and children captives to work gathering firewood, doing the cooking, hauling water, and tending the horses. The goblins leave the men's wagon locked and make several of the women carry small bowls of half-cooked meat and water to the prisoners. Turn to **140**.

7

You don't have any intention of waiting to see what the dragon has in mind. Instead you decide to make a dash back to the archway. Before Flamestrike's befuddled senses can react, you grab Kegan's hand and pull him after you past the huge switching tail. Willow dodges the dragon's feeble claws and follows you through the kitchen tunnel, just as a shrieking roar echoes around you. Turn to **80**.

8

The monster's talons are slashing at the mare's helpless body. The griffon has already ripped large gashes in her neck. The sight of the griffon's assault clears your mind of its sleepy haze, and you leap to your feet, wide awake. You know you'd be in great danger stranded in the wilderness without a horse, yet you also know that griffons are ferocious fighters. You're not sure you can fight such a powerful beast.

If you decide to try to escape, leaving the horse at the mercy of the griffon, turn to **160**. But if you decide to try to save your horse, turn to **180**.

9

Three times you have somehow managed to survive the dragon's choking fumes, but you haven't been able to get close enough to the beast for a clear strike with your sword. Finally the evil creature pauses and inhales deeply, preparing for a new assault with the deadly vapors.

You rush forward, Fireborn raised high, to take advantage of the dragon's pause. Just as you reach the monster's scaly neck, you hear an eerie chant behind you.

"Mystical mallet, smite this foe!"

Turn to **196**.

10

You find you're in a narrow passage leading straight ahead for perhaps a hundred feet, where it turns sharply to the left. A single door of tarnished bronze stands slightly ajar at the end of the next passage. You push it completely open and enter a perfectly round chamber with walls of carefully cut stone. Another door of bronze exactly like the one you've just come through is directly across the huge circular room, more than a hundred feet away.

In the center of the room, a gigantic chain slants upward, disappearing into the darkness of the seemingly roofless cylinder. The chain is anchored in the stone floor by a steel bracket three feet thick, and each link of the massive chain is larger than your entire body!

The four of you stare in silence at the emptiness of the chamber and marvel at the chain. Kegan's whispered expression of awe finally breaks the stillness. "What on Krynn could a chain that big be used for?" The walls of the chamber are so perfectly curved that his whisper echoes like a shout.

"Maybe we could find out if we climbed it!" answers Willow. In the light of Essa's spell, Willow's face is full of excitement, and you know that she's itching to discover what lies at the other end of the chain. Turn to **92**.

11

You continue to scout the flank of the wagon train from a hillside, until the wagons finally pull off at a wide mountain meadow. You dismount and watch as the goblins force the women and children out of their wagons. You recognize Kegan because of his size next to the other children and the women. The goblins force them to gather firewood and carry water from a swift stream cascading down the side of a cliff. Then two of the women are ordered to cook a hasty supper for the goblins and dragonmen.

Seeing your chance to reach the men's prison wagon, you slip behind the hungry guards into the blackness by the last wagon. The warriors from Solace recognize you immediately and beckon you closer to the bars.

"Can you pry the lock open with your dagger, Bern?" one of them whispers urgently.

"Can you get us weapons?" demands another.

"Maybe," you answer quickly, "but let's get this

21

door open first. Then we'll be able to—"

"Look out, Bern!" shouts one of the men. You duck instinctively as a spiked iron ball crashes against the bars of the wagon, mere inches above your head. The flail wraps around the bars, giving you time to drop down on one knee and draw Fireborn.

Before you stands a draconian, the studs of its leather armor gleaming in the moonlight. The powerful creature wrenches its weapon free from the bars and steps backward. You begin to circle each other cautiously. You've never fought a draconian before, and you're not sure of their weaknesses or strengths. Your fellow Solacians in the cage fall silent with fear as you wait for your opportunity to strike.

If you decide to fight the draconian, roll two dice to hit and add your fighting skill score to the total. If the result is 12 or more, turn to **29**. If your total is less than 12, deduct 4 hit points and turn to **53**.

You may elect to surrender to the draconian at any point during the action. If you do, turn to **117**. Finally, if you have at least 24 hit points, you can try to escape. Turn to **18**.

12

Your volcanic steel blade flashes viciously in the candlelight of Verminaard's bedchamber. You attack the three dragonmen with the fury of a berserker, slashing through their strong scale armor as if it were made of leather. The snarls and hisses of the draconians fill the room, and fear clouds their lidless eyes. Fireborn flies through the air as if it had a life of its own, striking death blows to two of the scaly monsters.

You whip the blade of volcanic steel away from their fallen bodies, expecting them to turn to statues of stone like their cousins. Instead, the gruesome remains of the winged creatures disintegrate into pools of an oily fluid that dissolves the monsters, armor, weapons, and all! The remaining draconian charges toward you, trying to force you into the acid pool! Turn to **123**.

13

When you reach the guardroom, Willow is already crouched by the small door, trying to pick a large padlock. It takes the skillful kender only a few seconds to open the lock, and soon you are all scrambling through the musty opening into a dark chamber. As you close the panel behind you, Kegan whispers excitedly in the darkness beside you.

"This will never work!" he cries. "They'll see that someone has opened the door and they'll know where we are!"

"I forgot about that!" says Willow's voice from somewhere nearby in the darkness. "Kegan's right!"

"I didn't forget," Essa interrupts. The small chamber suddenly fills with a soft white glow that surrounds the beautiful mage. She holds a tiny pouch in her hand and is removing a pinch of some kind of dried substance from the pouch. Flinging it at the panel, she utters a phrase in a strange language. For only an instant, the small door appears to quiver, then suddenly stops. A thin band of shimmering golden light encircles the frame. "Try to open it, Bern. You, too, Willow."

You test the panel, but it won't budge. Willow and Kegan press against it with you, but your combined weight and strength cannot force the magical seal to give way. You appear to be safe for the moment. You seize the chance to use Willow's healing medallion. Roll one die and add the result to your hit point total, then turn to **192**.

14

Pressing yourself back against the tree stump, you watch the hobgoblin officer drag Kegan's struggling body toward the other captives.

Your brother is larger than most ten-year-olds, and his adventures with you in the forests have hardened his young muscles. You smile at the gruff curses from the bulky hobgoblin as Kegan kicks his captor's hairy, unarmored shin. The officer flings the boy roughly to two of the goblins guarding the women and children, then growls a quick order. They bind Kegan's hands and feet, then leave him lying in the dust while they herd the other captives toward several wagons with stout iron bars. Turn to **82**.

15

With a loud groan, the rusted brackets snap off the outer wall under your combined weight. The three of you bound through the door into the open field behind Pax Tharkas. You close the door behind you and rehang the thick wooden beam so that no one will notice that it has been forced open.

In the distance, you can see yellowish smoke pouring from the mouth of the smelter cave just below the rim of the quarry. The tiny figures of slaves look like scurrying ants.

"Let's go! We've got to rescue the others!" Willow says excitedly.

"Wait a minute," you caution. "That's taking a big risk. Now that we're free ourselves, let's get out of here and bring back help for the others."

"You're making the decisions," Willow says with a shrug. "I'm just along for the fun."

If you want to try to rescue the others, as Willow suggests, turn to **83**. But if you feel that you and your companions should try to escape now, turn to **187**.

16

"Quick! Head for the tunnel!" you shout.

The four of you sprint toward the far end of the corridor. As you pass each of the stone slabs, more of the hideous zombies stumble from their crypts into Essa's magical light, seeking to stop the invaders of Kith-Kanan's tomb. Willow stops suddenly in the center of the corridor and flicks her kender hoopak twice, firing several of the deadly stones at the emerging zombies. The missiles strike the monsters with deadly accuracy, but they seem to have little effect on the gruesome creatures.

"Forget it, Willow! You can't kill something that's already dead with a hoopak!" you yell, grabbing her arm. "Get to the tunnel!"

Essa and Kegan have already reached the craggy opening when you pull the stubborn kender into the narrow passage. The elven mage presses her slender form against the rough wall and nods.

"Hurry past me," she says calmly. "I'll try to stop them."

You glance questioningly at the sorceress, but she turns away from your gaze with a look of trancelike concentration. Essa stares coldly at the sinister, shambling forms dragging their tattered, rotten limbs toward you. Suddenly her emerald eyes narrow as a force within her rises from her rigid shoulders into her throat, emerging in a long, low wail. At first the cry has no form, but then it assumes the sounds of the strange language of magic.

Turn to **61**.

17

The next sensation you feel is one of numbness in your leg, which is wedged between your body and a rough surface. You try to shift your weight off the leg, only to find that you're shackled by your wrists and ankles to a short chain.

As your brain clears, you see a small torch set in a bracket on the wall of the cavern. Its dim light floods over the damp walls and floor of the cell, revealing a small chamber with nothing but a light haze of smoke hanging above your head and the smell of sulphur in your nostrils. In the distance, you hear the sound of unrecognizable voices and the clanging of metal, and suddenly you know what has happened. You're chained to a wall in the iron quarries, without any hope of escaping. Willow and Kegan are nowhere in sight, and you can only hope that they have fared better than you. . . .

18

As the draconian stalks around you with its flail upraised, you glance at the light of the campfire only some twenty yards distant and realize that the goblins and the other draconian would be on top of you if you try to fight the dragonman. You glance to the side, where the mare is waiting in the shadows. If you can make it that far without being struck by the heavy spiked ball, you might be able to escape.

You wait until the draconian's winged back is

against the barred door of the prison wagon, then you take a vicious swipe with Fireborn, causing the dragonman to leap backward. The men inside the wagon have been watching every move, ready to help you. As soon as the draconian's wings press against the bars, strong hands grab the leathery skin and pull the wings inside the wagon. The creature shrieks with pain as you hear the crunching noise of the fragile bones in the wings breaking. The shouting and laughter from the campfire stops, and you see the shadows of quickly moving figures against the flickering firelight on the side of the wagons.

"Run, Bern!" someone shouts from inside the wagon. "Find help before they catch you, too!" Turn to **186**.

19

Filled with admiration for the courageous kender, you start to congratulate her. Just then, a door bursts open across the hall. Two large dragonmen, dressed in fine scale armor, peer into the hall. Their lidless eyes glaze when they see the bodies of the hobgoblins at your feet.

If you have less than 8 hit points remaining, you are too exhausted to continue fighting and you must surrender (turn to **193**). If you have 8 or more hit points left, you can leap across the guards' carcasses and into Verminaard's throne room (turn to **199**).

"It's no use looking here any more, Essa," you tell the sorceress. "If there's a secret door here, we can't find it. Our best bet is to start over again from the cellar. Maybe the secret route to the Sla-Mori is there."

"I agree with Bern," Willow says, noticing the elf's puzzled look. "Come on, before those scaly guards find a way to get past your magical seal on the door! We need your light spell to show us the way."

You retrace your steps quickly until you're back at the cellar door. Willow pulls the hidden lever, and you all begin to search the same wall for another secret entrance. The pounding on the door to the guardroom is louder, and the voices of the draconians have become angrier. Despite your efforts, no one can find a trace of a crack in the solid stone. Turn to **95**.

21

You swing your sword mightily. It strikes the dragonman's armor a glancing blow, knocking the breath from the creature's body. But before you can follow up with a killing blow, you are struck from behind by the second dragonman. You topple to the ground unconscious. Roll one die for damage, subtract the number from your total hit points, then turn to **114**.

22

You put your shoulder against the door and push with all your might. At first nothing happens, but gradually you feel the bar begin to give. Suddenly the doors burst open, and you tumble out into the bright sunlight.

You're in a courtyard behind the fortress. Not far away, you can see goblin and hobgoblin guards barking orders to slaves in the quarries, but they don't seem to have noticed you yet.

Carefully you close the doors and, crouching low, make your way along the wall toward the foothills you see rising in the distance, off to the side of one of the quarry openings. After several tense minutes, you gain the slope and soon find yourself under cover of thick forest. You've made it!

Thankful to have escaped this grim fortress with your life, you resolve, somehow, to return with help and free the other prisoners of Pax Tharkas if it's the last thing you do. . . .

As a reward for escaping from Pax Tharkas with your life, you may add one extra experience point to your score the next time you play the adventure.

23

The elk that draw the caravan wagons are near exhaustion by the time the wagons near Gateway. In the failing light of dusk, the goblin teamsters rein their animals to a halt on the outskirts of the devastated town. You shudder as you realize that the mysterious red dragons have scorched the Plains of Abanasinia as well as the valley of Crystalmir.

As you watch the firelight in the distance, you decide that it would be better to follow the caravan to its final destination so that you may have an opportunity to learn more about these mysterious, frightening events that seem to threaten all of Ansalon. Still, you might have a better chance to rescue the prisoners if you surprise the goblins on the first night, but then you'd know only as much about the dragons as you do now.

If you decide to change your mind and attack now, turn to **140**. If you choose to continue following the caravan, turn to **146**.

24

"Not so fast, Willow," you warn her. "We still haven't explored the passage at the end of this hall. It may be wiser to take the more obvious route."

"Well, make up your mind quick!" croaks Kegan. "Those slabs are starting to move again!"

You twist around just as the nearest crypt door is starting to slide open with a groaning noise. The zombies are renewing their attack!

If you want to look for the carrion crawler's tunnel, turn to **158**. If you decide to run for the passage at the end of the zombie corridor, turn to **16**.

25

"Perhaps we can talk our way out of this somehow!" you mumble to Willow. "If we can convince Flamestrike that we're friends, she may not sound an alarm!"

"Sure. This ought to be fun! By all means, let's try to make friends with the dragon," Willow says with a grin.

"Be quiet, and both of you be ready to back up my story," you murmur impatiently, stepping in front of the large beast. Turn to **179**.

26

"Look, Willow, or whatever your name is," you say irritably. "This conversation is getting us absolutely nowhere. I wish you'd—" Suddenly another wave of dizziness sweeps over you, and the last thing you see as you drift into unconsciousness is the hurt expression in the girl's wide kender eyes.

You awaken with the sharp smell of sulphur in your nose. You try to shift your arms and legs to a more comfortable position, but to your amazement, you find you can't move. You look around to discover that they're shackled to a stone wall. You seem to be in some sort of a dark cave, and in the distance, you can hear metallic clanking sounds, as of metal tools against rock. You decide you must be held prisoner in a mine of some sort.

Your head is throbbing terribly as your mind turns to the kender girl. You wonder where she is, and what would have happened to you if you had heard her out. At any rate, she can't be worse off than you, because unless some miracle happens, it looks like you'll spend your last days shackled to the wall somewhere in a dismal mine. . . .

27

The draconians pour into the bedchamber so quickly that escape is impossible! There are seven of the large creatures, all wearing armor and brandishing polished broadswords. These are the Dragon

Highlord's personal bodyguards, and you see quickly that it would be useless to fight them.

You pitch the chest of potions onto the bed, diverting their attention long enough to unroll the small parchment from Verminaard's desk. The language is ancient Common, spoken by legal scholars and other sages in Haven. You begin to read aloud from the discolored scroll, stumbling over some of the words that you can't understand.

" 'By these words, O mighty Anthraxus, know that thy loyal servant calls upon thy magnificent power to vanquish his enemies before you! Visit thy terrible wrath upon those who would seek to silence thy priest. . . .' "

"Stop, Bern!" yells Willow. "You're summoning Verminaard's demonic protector!" Turn to **49**.

28

Trembling, you begin to explore the cold, dark chamber.

"There! In the corner!" yells Kegan suddenly.

In the darkest alcove of the cavern, a shadowy form has detached itself from the deeper blackness of the rocky wall. It looks like a swirling fog of dark vapors as it forms itself into the shape of a spectral being with a head and arms. Pinpoints of red light flare suddenly into eyes as the creature's body gradually assumes a more material appearance.

"A wraith!" Essa gasps in horror. You sweep Fireborn from its sheath and step forward.

"No, Bern! You can't stop a wraith with a normal weapon!" warns the sorceress. "It's the undead spirit of an evil person. You must fight it with an enchanted blade! Use my sword!"

The elven mage has already whipped the magical weapon from her belt. Its silver glare shines brighter than Essa's aura as she flings it to you across the chamber. You catch the sword by its crystal hilt, astonished to feel how light it is. The smooth handle tingles in your hand as if it were alive.

Suddenly you feel a cold blast of air as the wraith rushes toward the four of you in the center of the cavern.

If you decide to fight the wraith, roll two dice to hit and add the result to your fighting skill score. If the total is 11 or more, turn to **44**. If it is less than 11, subtract 7 hit points and turn to **166**.

If you decide to retreat from the wraith, turn to **150**. The wraith will immediately drain your life energy if you try to surrender.

29

The draconian hisses in pain as your sword strikes its left wing. It tries to flap the leathery appendage to move out of your range, but the bleeding wing is helpless. You rush forward, taking full advantage of the creature's wound, and slash furiously at its neck. Fireborn's steel edge bites deep into the reptilian's hide, stifling its cry before it can alert the others gathered around the campfire.

The draconian's horrified eyes become glassy, and it seems to freeze instantly, its gruesome face upturned to the starlight. You feel a strange sensation from the leather hilt of your sword and realize that the blade is stuck fast in the gaping neck wound!

The draconian has turned into a stone statue of some kind, and Fireborn is caught fast inside it! You stare at it in wonder, completely forgetting your purpose.

"Quick, Bern! The door!" The hushed whisper from the prison wagon reminds you of your mission. You tear your eyes away from the frozen draconian and resume your attempt to open the lock. The point of your dagger is slender enough to enter the large key-hole, and you're finally able to force open the lock. Turn to **111**.

30

Wasting no time, you seize the hobgoblin by its sweaty tunic and drag it through the doorway out into the dark hall. You know it's still hours before daylight comes to Pax Tharkas, and most of the guards are still asleep. Pulling the hobgoblin's unconscious form to the nearest corner, you quickly unbuckle the officer's sword belt and fasten it around your own waist. You begin to dart down the hall, then stop, undecided. You might escape Pax Tharkas yourself and try to find help. Perhaps the elves in their hidden land could be persuaded to help you. But that would mean you'd have to leave Kegan behind.

If you decide to try to escape from Pax Tharkas now, turn to **118**. But if you decide to find Kegan first, then think about escape, turn to **47**.

31

You whisper your plan to Kegan and clasp his shoulder. "Can you do it?"

"Just watch me and be ready!" he replies confidently. Then he fills the bucket and hurries toward the campsite. The guards don't notice him until he reaches the tethered elk at the far end of the camp. Then one of them widens its glassy eyes and yells.

"Hey, you! Boy! Bring that water quick!"

As soon as Kegan reaches the cluster of rowdy goblins, he throws the heavy oaken bucket into the campfire, scattering sparks and ashes everywhere and startling the drunken creatures to their feet. Kegan darts into the shadows behind the grazing elk and disappears into the darkness of the trees on the side of the camp opposite you.

The goblins scream a string of curses, and a large hobgoblin and two draconians emerge from a large tent nearby. You see that the leathery wings of the dragonmen are now unfurled, fanning the air. They're crouched on all four limbs, moving rapidly, with the aid of their wings, toward the forest in pursuit of Kegan.

Quickly you sneak to one of the prison wagons hold-

ing the men and begin to pry on the lock with your dagger. Recognizing you, the men watch silently. Suddenly one cries, "Bern, look out behind you!"

Whirling around, you stare into the slobbering muzzles of a brace of huge war dogs, and your heart fills with dread. You know that war dogs are trained killers, protected by a thin layer of studded leather and a wide collar with needle spikes.

You draw Fireborn, hoping to kill the beasts before their masters return to discover your trick. Both war dogs crouch and spring at you at once, snarling and snapping their massive jaws at your throat.

You've only an instant to decide what to do. If you decide to fight the war dogs, roll two dice to hit and add your fighting skill score to the dice roll. If the total is 10 or more, turn to **127**. If the total is less than 10, subtract 2 hit points and turn to **37**. Remember that you can try to hit the war dogs more than once, just as long as you deduct 2 hit points each time you miss.

If you have 26 hit points or more, you can try to run from the war dogs at any point during the action. Turn to **156**. It is impossible to surrender. The war dogs would tear out your throat if you tried.

32

"Look there—at the bottom!" you cry. Kegan wedges the thin blade of his knife into a slit where the wall joins the floor of the corridor. The excited boy scrapes the blade along the bottom edge of the wall, dislodging a line of ancient clay that was used to conceal the bottom crack of a disguised door. Willow rushes to the wall to look for the door's outline along the wall or a release mechanism.

"Here's another crack!" she whispers. Soon the secret door is outlined in the magical light. It extends all the way to the top of the corridor and fills it from side to side. But there's no sign of any way to open the disguised panel.

"Step away from it," suggests Essa. You all move behind the sorceress as she reaches into her pouch for an ingredient for a spell. Brushing her disheveled silver hair from her face, the sorceress concentrates intensely on the wall of stone. The elf's loveliness hardens, and her eyes narrow to vivid green slits.

She steps forward and uses some reddish powder to mark a mystical sign on the wall. Then she shouts the same short phrase three times in rapid succession. On the last syllable, the beautiful mage reaches out and knocks lightly on the magical symbol. Turn to **122**.

33

The strange draconians are a total mystery to you. You have never seen them anywhere in the Crystalmir valley before. Solace seems to have been destroyed overnight by some powerful evil force of which Toede's ugly goblin horde is only a small contingent. You wonder what the old woman saw in the night skies to imagine them to be dragons. You want to know why your peaceful town has been razed and why many of its citizens, including Kegan, have been taken prisoner. The only thing you can do is follow the caravan and try to understand these terrible events and do whatever you can to undo them. You know you can't follow on foot. The caravan would get too far ahead. You need a horse, but they're scarce in Solace. Turn to **81**.

34

Just as the hobgoblin and its two gully dwarf servants start to march you and the other men into the slave pits, you push one of the dwarves into his master's path. The wretched little creature tumbles beneath the hobgoblin's boots, tripping the oafish monster. Before it can recover from the surprise and pick itself up, you race from the trail toward the rugged cliffside near the smelter.

Roll one die to see if your escape is successful. Add your physical prowess score to the dice roll. If the total is 6 or more, turn to **72**. If it is less than 6, turn to **170**.

35

"The gully dwarves' quarters are this way." Turning to the right, Willow leads the way down the corridor. Soon you come to another hallway with a single door. You crouch at the panel and hear sounds of laughter as well as what sounds like the crashes of furniture from the other side.

"What's that?" you ask Willow.

"Just your friends," she replies with mock sweetness. "Having a quiet breakfast, I suppose. Shall we join them?" You frown at her and push on the door.

"Look out!" exclaims Kegan, pushing you to one side. Turn to **109**.

36

"We have come all the way from Solace with important news!" you reply, determined to remain calm. "This youth is the son of Hobarth Vallenshield, the legendary warrior from Solace. I've learned something from him for Lord Verminaard's ears only!"

The two guards glance first at Kegan, then at each other. Their beady black eyes gleam fiercely against their yellowish skin as they silently decide whether to believe you. Finally the guard on the left nods its head toward a door at the end of the corridor.

"Take the child to the master's private quarters. As soon as his lordship is finished with his business, I'll tell him why you're here and send for you."

You must decide quickly whether to accept this suggestion. You think you might have a slim chance of surprising the hobgoblins and forcing your way past them into the throne room, but it might be wiser to tell them you'll wait.

If you elect to wait in Verminaard's private quarters, turn to **181**. If you decide to attack the guards, turn to **62**.

Your adventures as a Ranger in the forests of Crystalmir have prepared you for a confrontation with war dogs. No matter how well trained these animals may be, you doubt if they could rival the ferocity of a dire wolf, and you've faced those creatures alone before and lived to tell about it.

Both war dogs leap at the same time. You do exactly what they don't expect you to do—you rush toward them and dive under them! The surprised animals sail over you, but not before you slash the larger one in its hindquarters with your sword. The injured beast's yelp brings its dragonman master scrambling from the campfire faster than you thought anything could move. This is the first time you've ever seen a draconian charge, its leathery wings lifting its armored bulk forward in long, distance-consuming hops.

As you watch in horror, the draconian draws its long, curved sword. You realize—as you hear a low growl from behind you—that you have made a fatal mistake. You forgot the other war dog! You feel its bulk crash onto your back and sink its long fangs into your neck! Before the great jaws crush your spine, you see the draconian's lipless mouth curl in a sinister sneer. . . .

"No!" you say sternly, putting your hand on the kender's wrist. "This has gone far enough, Willow! Just once in your life, be serious! We're in real danger here!"

"How dare you order me around, Bern Vallenshield?" Willow yells, forgetting where she is.

Just then, the door swings open and the two hobgoblins enter. "What's going on here?" one says, its eyes widening. "Rummaging through Lord Verminaard's things? Wait until he hears about this!"

There's no choice now. You must fight these two monsters. Turn to **62**.

39

"While we're here, we might as well explore as much as we can," you tell Essa. "I have complete confidence in Willow's skill as a handler. You stay here with Kegan. That way, we'll have enough light to check the door for traps before we open it, and you two would be left to get help if something happens."

"I want to go, too, Bern!" your brother complains. You look at his disappointed frown and smile.

"Come on, then," you agree. "But stay out of the way while Willow and I are examining that door."

"I'll go along, too. You may just need help of another kind," Essa says in her quiet way. The beautiful elf follows behind Kegan, and you all approach the second bronze door cautiously.

You're still more than ten feet away from the door's metal surface when suddenly the solid stone floor vanishes from beneath your feet! In the instant before you are crushed on the rocks far below, the cries of your brother and your two courageous women companions mingle in your last thoughts. . . .

40

In Essa's magical light, you see a narrow passage cutting through the debris of a rockslide, perhaps the residue of a cave-in during the Cataclysm. The rough tunnel leads to a dead end.

"There has to be an opening somewhere around here," says Essa. The four of you examine the rock wall in front of you for anything resembling a door.

"Here it is!" you exclaim suddenly. "Kegan, give

me your knife!" You push the blade into a thin crack running from the ceiling to the floor of the cavern.

"Let me try to open it!" says Willow. The kender passes her sensitive fingers over the rock surface until she locates a small round depression. "Hand me that butcher knife," she mutters. With its tip, she scrapes some dried mud away from a hole, enlarging it until she can reach inside. "There's a lever of some kind in here!" she exclaims. Suddenly the crack widens as the slab of stone shifts to one side with a grinding sound. Turn to **4**.

Turn to **4**.

41

"Don't!" Willow warns quickly. "The drawer's trapped with a poisoned needle! Let me do it." She lifts the carved ebony case from the drawer with the greatest care, scarcely breathing all the while. When her hands are clear of the drawer, she takes a deep breath and offers the small chest to you.

"They're potions, but I don't know what kind," she warns. "The two milky ones may be healing oils, since white's a common color for medicines, but I've never seen anything like the dark red potion."

"They must be valuable if Verminaard hid them in a trapped drawer!" mutters Kegan excitedly. Willow smiles at your brother and nods.

"Either that or he put them there and forgot about them," Willow says, shrugging. "At any rate, he obviously isn't interested in them or he would have used them long ago. I'll just take them along."

Groaning, you shake your head, knowing better than to try to argue with a kender. Nervously you keep your eyes on the door while Willow continues to search the room as if she didn't have a care in the world.

The kender approaches the second locked door and

opens it as easily as the first. Posting Kegan as guard in the dining hall, you follow Willow into the next room. When you enter, you see that you're in a huge bedchamber. A magnificent canopied bed fills one whole end of the spacious room. Against the opposite wall, you see a massive desk, covered with parchments and scrolls.

Willow is scanning a map of some kind on the desktop as you enter the room.

"This is Verminaard's plan of battle!" she says excitedly. "He seems to be focusing most of his attack on Qualinesti!"

You start to share the kender's excitement and begin rummaging through the scrolls and papers on the desk for more details. You start to untie a faded red ribbon on one of the smaller parchments, but once more Willow stops you.

"Be careful what you read in a cleric's study," she warns. "Especially scrolls like that. I don't know what dark forces Verminaard serves, but sometimes they can be summoned by anyone who reads cursed scrolls!"

The kender's warning gives you a sense of foreboding. Before you can ask her more questions about such powerful scrolls, Kegan bursts through the door with a look of alarm in his dark, bright eyes.

"Dragonmen!" he cries. "Let's get out of here!"

But the warning comes too late. The doorway fills with the winged monsters, each brandishing a shortsword and wearing splinted armor. They crowd into their master's bedchamber, weapons drawn. You have time for only one action before they will be upon you.

If you decide to fight the draconians, turn to **60**. If you choose to drink one of the potions, turn to **145**. If you elect to read the scroll in your hand, turn to **27**.

You dream of a huge winged creature that breathes a terrible stream of fire at you. Amid your troubled dreams, you roll your head against a rough boulder, waking from your disturbed slumber. You're not certain in your groggy state, but you think you heard a frightened whinny from the mare. You remember tying her to a twisted tree root near the stream so that she could have her fill of drink while she rests. Raising your head, you see that dawn is only minutes away.

In the semidarkness, a huge black shadow hovers in the brightening sky above the tethered horse. You recognize the beast immediately from stories you have heard from other Rangers. The creature has the hindquarters of a lion and the head of a giant bird of prey—a griffon!

Turn to **8**.

43

The three of you turn away from the door to the entry hall and move as quickly and as quietly as possible back the way you came. The corridor seems twice as long as before, perhaps because you repeatedly glance nervously over your shoulder. Finally you reach the opposite door with no sign of movement from the other end of the corridor. Willow has already opened the door when you reach the first tower, and you dart through it into the carpeted hallway.

"We know the playroom's a dead end," you murmur. "Our only other chance seems to be to hide in the cellar and wait until night to make our escape."

"Or we could try to learn more about Verminaard's plans," Willow adds, a tinge of excitement in her voice. "His quarters are just around the corner of the hallway, beyond the kitchen."

You're finding it difficult to distinguish bravery from recklessness in many of the girl's suggestions, but this one has some merit. If you do manage to escape from the fortress, the more you know about the Dragon Highlord's intentions, the better your chances to stop him.

If you decide to hide downstairs and wait for nightfall to try to escape, turn to **131**. But if you choose to spy on Verminaard, turn to **121**.

44

The sorceress's magical sword flashes again and again through the wispy body of the wraith. Each time the evil being attacks, your muscles become numb with cold. It feels as if your strength is being drained away, so that you're barely able to lift even this light enchanted weapon. You fight your growing exhaustion and continue your assault on the spectral creature.

You maintain the fury of your attack until finally some of the wraith's material substance appears to be fading. Encouraged, you lunge at the monster with renewed energy. At the same time, Willow steps closer to try hitting the wraith with a stone from her hoopak. The missile merely passes through the wraith's shadowy form.

Essa's enchanted blade strikes the undead spirit again and again, weakening its outline even more. Then you notice that a strange thing is happening to Willow's healing talisman. Each time you score a hit on the wraith, the medallion glows more brightly.

"Use your talisman, Willow! The wraith's strength is failing!" you cry.

The kender glances at the carved disk hanging from her neck and understands what you mean immediately. She holds the medallion at arm's length and stalks toward the disintegrating creature. The talisman is a dazzling purple light by the time she reaches the wraith and thrusts the medallion toward it. Turn to **136**.

45

The goblins grin evilly and point excitedly toward your steel blade. They begin to chatter, and you suspect they're arguing over who will get your sword. One of the creatures grabs Fireborn from your hand and another raises its spear. You hold your empty hands up weakly in surrender.

The goblin with the spear snarls something unintelligible and whips the butt of its shaft into your stomach. You double over, the breath forced from your lungs. You never see the crashing blow as the cowardly monster slams the spear shaft against your head. Roll one die for damage and subtract the number from your total hit points, then turn to **114**.

46

"The women's prison is probably our best bet," you reply. "Lead the way!"

Willow nods and turns down a corridor ten feet wide that leads to the right. At the end of the corridor, you see a well-worn door of heavy wood and another hallway branching off to the right.

"That's where the gully dwarves sleep," she says, motioning to the right, "and this is a guardroom. We have to go through here to get to my cellblock."

"Guardroom? You didn't say anything about a guardroom!" you exclaim.

"In the daytime, the draconians are usually upstairs, drinking and gambling in the room across from Verminaard's council chamber. He uses them as his personal bodyguards whenever he leaves this tower, and he wants them close by. They're never around here during the day."

"I hope you're right. I'd hate to have to fight our way *into* prison!" you exclaim, tightening your grip on Fireborn as you follow the kender into the guardroom. You notice a smaller door, with a large padlock on it, straight ahead. "What's that?"

"A storage cellar. There's nothing in there but some old junk. That's where they made us put everybody's extra stuff when they brought us here from Solace. But there's no place to hide in there!" she adds quickly.

You nod and push Kegan behind Willow into a very narrow passage, with a bare wall on the left and three more barred doors on the right. As soon as you're inside, you hear the sound of women's voices.

"It's Willow!" "What's going on out there, Willow?"

The kender stops at the first door, where several women are crowding their faces against the bars. You recognize some of them as being from Solace.

"Look! It's Bern and Kegan Vallenshield!" "Bern! Can you help us?"

When Willow opens the cell door, the women surround you, barraging you with a flurry of questions about their husbands and kinsmen. Several of the older women take Kegan aside, anxious to mother the boy. Your brother twists his face in disgust, but you notice that he doesn't push them away. You can tell that he's enjoying the attention, although he's trying to act as if he's too old for it.

"We can talk later!" you tell them. "Right now we have to hide! Verminaard's men will be here in a matter of minutes looking for us!" Turn to **191**.

You decide that the first thing you must do is to find out where the children are being held. You know they must be in this part of the fortress somewhere, but you don't want to risk getting caught searching for them. Settling down in a hidden corner, you decide to wait until morning.

Day is just dawning when you suddenly hear the sound of voices nearby. Peering around a corner, you see a small group of women climbing up a staircase. Among them, you recognize Willow Lighthand, the kender girl whose strange medallion healed your wounds in the slave wagon.

She's with a group of ten women led by Maritta, the seamstress from Solace, and they appear to be headed for the kitchen. They nearly shout out in alarm when they see you burst from the shadows. "Bern Vallenshield!" "How is my husband?" "Have you seen—"

"Shhh!" you hiss, silencing the excited women. "There's no time to talk. I have to find my brother and get out of here to get help! Have any of you seen him?"

The Solacian women glance nervously at each other, as if unwilling to answer.

"What is it?" you demand in a harsh whisper. "Where is Kegan? Has anything happened to him?"

The kender girl looks at the frightened women and leans toward Maritta with a toss of her coppery braids.

"Go on to the kitchen," she says in her husky voice. "I'll take him to his brother!"

The seamstress frowns but nods. "Try to hurry, child. That poor old creature is more suspicious than my mother ever was, rest her soul!"

"Your people were right," Willow whispers as soon

as you're alone. "Your town *was* attacked by red dragons. One of the beasts now guards the children of Solace, and your brother is among them!"

"Willow, have you heard anything about someone called Verminaard?" you demand.

"Verminaard is an evil cleric who controls the red dragons of Pax Tharkas," the kender replies immediately. "I haven't seen him, but his chambers are nearby, just across from the kitchen. His bodyguards are dragonmen, but not the same kind we saw in the caravan. These creatures are taller than the Baaz draconians, and they fight with poisoned weapons."

"Take me to Kegan!" you urge the kender. "But first, let me find you a weapon of some kind." You turn to search the hobgoblin's body, but Willow stops you.

"You don't need to do that. Look!" The girl is beaming, her white teeth shining against her deeply tanned face. She has a curious weapon in her hand, one that you've seen only twice before. It's a homemade, cut-down version of a kender hoopak—the combination bullet sling and fighting stick favored by the kenders for either close or distant combat!

Grinning at the resourceful kender, you follow her leather-clad form into the main hallway, which was once a luxurious room. A thick carpet of purple wool, soiled with countless muddy bootprints, blends softly with rich tapestries of deep crimson and gold on the walls. The peaceful embroidered scenes of elven and dwarvish nobility have been marred by crude slogans and drawings, some rather lewd. There are three doors of heavy vallenwood, all scarred and initialed, leading from the hall, and one long carpeted corridor. Willow nods her head toward one of the doors.

"This is the children's playroom," she whispers,

opening the heavy panel and waiting for you to follow her.

You find yourself inside a large empty room with crude rag dolls, hand-carved wagons, and other homemade toys scattered about the floor. A pair of heavy double doors are set in an alcove on your right, flanked on either side by two heavily barred windows. You remember seeing these windows from the outside, and you recall that the doors are secured by a thick wooden beam on the other side of the second tower. To the left, you see a smaller door of polished vallenwood and an archway leading into darkness.

"Come on," says Willow. "The children are napping in the room beyond Flamestrike's chamber."

You follow the kender through the archway into a dimly lit stone tunnel that has been made into a kitchen. Against the right-hand wall, long rows of shelves contain small barrels of salted meat, dried beans, salt, potatoes, and other foodstuffs. To your left, you see a huge wood stove and a long counter cluttered with pots, pans, and other cooking utensils. Willow is waiting for you at the opposite end of the tunnel. She is pressing her hand to her lips, motioning for you to be silent. Clutching Fireborn's hilt, you join Willow and look into the next room. Turn to **161**.

48

Once your sleeve has been torn away from the griffon's talons, you swing Fireborn with all your strength at the monster's leg. The razor-edged blade cuts into the feathered foreleg, severing an artery. The creature's dark blood spouts into the cold air, drenching you in its sticky warmth. The griffon's whole body jerks reflexively as it tries to tear your arm off with its hawkish beak.

You twist away from the sharp mouth, swinging your blade as hard as you can at the monster's throat. Its thick feathers cause your blow to glance aside, but the griffon's wings have begun to flap more slowly. Blood still gushes from the wound in its foreleg, and you know the creature is getting weaker. You glance below to the snowy fields and craggy peaks of the mountain range, hoping that the monster will somehow be able to land safely before it dies from loss of blood. Turn to **164**.

49

The kender's warning comes too late. The Dragon Highlord's inner chamber fills with a fetid odor too horrible to name. The wall hangings begin to flutter, although you feel no breeze blowing across your face. From an unknown plane, you hear a distant wheezing sound. The wheezing grows steadily louder until words begin to take form in your brain. Between you and the guards, a shimmering figure appears from nowhere, acquiring more substance every moment. Suddenly the scroll bursts into flame, burning to ashes in seconds.

"You're a fool, human!" thunders a horrible, mocking voice. As your eyes recover from the blinding flash of the exploding parchment, you see the terrible face of the speaker. Its material form appears to be

that of a tall human dressed in tattered gray clothes, rotten and moldy with the stench of the grave. But even more loathsome is the demon's head.

Instead of a man's head, the demon has the head of a diseased ram. Its skin is stretched taut over the bestial face, broken by fissures and sores that ooze pus and blood over the filthy wool of the muzzle. The demon's black horns are curled forward, almost meeting above its shining amber eyes.

"Death and eternal servitude come quickly to one who calls Anthraxus the Decayed from his domain without such simple precautions as a pentagram! Come to me, mortal! Now!"

You are powerless to resist the demon's mental control. You hear Willow scream somewhere in the background of your stolen mind, but her words are meaningless. You step forward, to be enveloped by the powerful arms of the oinodaemon, and feel its rotten flesh take you to your new master's kingdom on the Lower Plane.

50

"That was a close call!" Kegan exclaims.

"Look at that!" you whisper, turning around. The zombies have vanished back into their crypts. All trace of your passage is obliterated!

"So that's how the elves guard their king!" Essa says in awe. "Now the Royal Guard lie in wait for the next who attempt to enter."

Willow looks with wide eyes at her medallion. "This is really something!" she says. Then she looks at you and grins. "Well, let's move on. I'm getting bored."

"Bored!" you exclaim, still shivering from your encounter with the undead guardians. "If you're so bored, why don't you—"

"Just a joke, Bern!" laughs the kender. "Still, I think we should look for some way out of this corridor. Perhaps we should just go back to the hall with the granite columns and explore that other door."

"And have to pass through here again?" you cry. "You, maybe, but not me! Opening those two doors may have been what woke up the zombies, and I'm not taking that chance again!"

"Bern may be right," Essa agrees gently. "The elves and dwarves who built the Sla-Mori were master craftsmen, and they sometimes used magic in their designs. There may be more hidden passages in this hallway, perhaps behind one of these slabs."

"Do you mean inside one of the crypts?" demands Kegan with a horrified look. "With the zombies?"

"It's a possibility," says Essa. "We know Willow's medallion can turn them. They won't harm us as long as she's with us."

"You may have something there, Essa!" exclaims the kender. "If we don't find another secret passage, we can always head for the tunnel at the end of this corridor."

"Well, let's get busy," you say quickly. "If we haven't found anything within a few minutes, we'll take the tunnel. But be careful, and be sure to yell out if you see or hear anything!"

Roll one die to try to find the secret door and add it to your observation skill score. If the total is 6 or more, turn to **106**. If it is less then 6, turn to **102**.

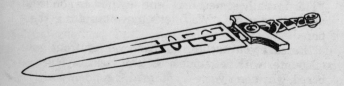

56

The guards are much better fighters than you hoped. They drop their pikes and draw longswords, weapons made of steel mined and smelted in the quarries of Pax Tharkas and worked into razor-edged blades of excellent hardness. You try to parry their thrusts and slashes with Fireborn, but you take several painful hits on your legs and arms. From the corner of your eye, you see Willow being stormed by one of the creatures. The brave kender girl falls backward, swinging her hoopak like a club against the armored monster.

Suddenly Kegan leaps on the guard's back, trying to help Willow. The large monster flings your brother against the wall and raises its sword, ready to cleave Kegan's skull. Turn to **113**.

"Here!" Willow's sudden gasp startles you. The kender is crouched by one of the crypt slabs only about forty feet from the double doors. You all crowd around her, letting Essa direct her magical light closer to the floor. Sure enough, there are no traces of movement whatsoever in the dust by the slab.

"Either this one's empty, or the zombie inside is awfully sound asleep!" Willow says in her throaty whisper. "Let's open it!"

"Not so fast!" you tell the fearless but reckless kender. Drawing Fireborn, you raise the blade above your head in front of the slab. "Now!"

Willow and Kegan pull as hard as they can on the iron ring, expecting heavy resistance. Instead, the stone swings outward easily, causing your brother and the girl to lose their balance and fall on their backs with a muffled crash. In the light of Essa's spell, the entrance to the crypt is filled suddenly with the terrible head of a huge insectlike creature!

"It's a carrion crawler!" you gasp, dodging the monster's writhing tentacles and flashing mandibles. You strike the armored head of the carnivorous beast with Fireborn as it tries to lunge forward out of the crypt.

If you choose to fight the monster, roll two dice to hit, then add your fighting skill score to the total. If the resulting number is 13 or more, turn to **67**. If it is less than 13, subtract 3 hit points and turn to **129**.

If you decide to retreat from the crawler instead, turn to **139**. This carrion crawler has eaten only a few dried zombies in the past several decades and is starving. It will eat you if you try to surrender.

53

Slowly the dragonman circles around you, swinging the flail loosely in its scaly hand. It's nearly a foot shorter than you are and wearing studded leather armor. Its dark wings are fluttering lightly, although there's no wind blowing. You're about to charge the creature when suddenly it drops to the ground on all four limbs and flaps its wings wildly. Its movement is so sudden that you don't have time to sidestep its charge, and the creature is on top of you instantly, swinging the heavy flail.

The spiked ball explodes against your bare head, blinding you with a crushing pain. You vaguely remember the yells of the men in the prison wagon just before you slip into blackness. Roll one die for damage, subtract the result from your hit points, then turn to **114**.

54

"Let's get out of here!" Willow shouts, guiding Kegan around the spreading pools of corrosive gore. You leap easily across the sizzling puddles and follow the kender and your brother into the next room.

You have barely reached the dining chamber when the effects of the potion suddenly vanish as quickly as they came, leaving you exhausted. The room seems to be swirling, and you have to catch yourself on the large table to keep from fainting.

"Steady, Bern!" says Willow. "We need you to help us get out of this place!" The kender wraps both her arms around you and eases you gently to the floor. Her healing medallion brushes the skin of your cheek, causing it to tingle pleasantly.

"Put the talisman over my head, Willow," you whisper, scarcely having the strength to talk. The girl nods and slips the medallion around your neck. You have one healing throw. Roll one die, add it to your hit point total, then turn to **194**.

55

Despite her words, the fearless kender takes out her hoopak and flings a barrage of stones into the mass of monsters. The missiles make sickening thumping noises as they bury themselves in the rotting flesh of the oncoming zombies. You see small holes suddenly appear in their gruesome foreheads as the hoopak stones find their marks, but the zombies continue their relentless march toward you.

You slash at one of the fearsome creatures with your sword, hitting it squarely, but the steel blade passes right through it! All the legends you've ever heard about zombies leap to your mind, and it occurs to you that these aren't behaving like zombies at all! There must be a powerful magic affecting everything in this room!

Do you still wish to continue to fight? If you do, turn to 88. But you also have another idea of how you might get out of here. If you decide to try it, turn to 73. (You'll find a clue in 98.)

56

The battle is a short, vengeful slaughter of the drunken goblins and their draconian companions.

You hear a low growl and turn just as the last draconian releases a brace of armored war dogs in an attempt to cover its escape. The fierce animals are far more formidable opponents than the goblins, but you and your men quickly surround and kill them. You whirl around just as the dragonman's dark wings disappear in the distant shadows of the cliff. One of the former prisoners notches an arrow in his shortbow, but you raise your hand to stop him.

"Don't waste your shaft," you tell him. "We have a long way to travel, with many mouths to feed."

"You can't just let it get away!" cries a voice at your side. You see Kegan standing beside you with a desperate expression on his twelve-year-old face. "It was with the monsters who burned Solace!"

"We don't know how many reinforcements may be waiting in the shadows ahead, Kegan," you tell your brother. "They mentioned a place called Pax Tharkas, a place I've never heard of before tonight. We need to find someone who can tell us more about these mountains before we can face the powerful force that summoned the dragons, and we'll need more than just a few men, Kegan. But I swear before all of you that we will put an end to this evil that has come to Krynn!" As reward for your bravery, you may give yourself one extra experience point the next time you play this adventure.

57

The draconians recover from their surprise more quickly than you hoped. They form a line across the cramped room, thrusting savagely with their broadswords. You try to hold them off with Fireborn, but you take several painful slashes on your arm and side. With a sinking feeling, you realize that you're outnumbered by the monsters and must retreat before they overwhelm you.

"Get back!" you yell. "We can't hold them!"

You guard the door with vicious swipes of your blade while Willow and Kegan make their way out the door behind you. Then you back out of the entry hall and slam the door.

"Run for the other tower!" yells Willow. "I'll cover you!" Turn to **5**.

58

Quickly you glance up and down the road, but you don't see anything moving. The only thing you've heard is that hoarse, warning cry. You hurry down the road toward Solace, ignoring the hidden voice. You must find out what happened to your home and your younger brother.

You have not gone far, however, when suddenly two figures, heavily caped and hooded, leap out of the woods and grab you roughly. Turn to **134**.

59

"Others have been here before us," you whisper. "There are tracks of some small creatures—rats, I think—going both ways. And there are tracks of larger creatures—maybe draconians."

"The larger creatures must have come in from the outside!" Willow exclaims in a husky whisper. "If we can follow them back to where they came in, we might find a way out of here!"

You push your way past the kender girl, with Kegan on your heels. Your brother is already an excellent tracker and has helped you follow such trails in the forests above Crystalmir. Together you crouch close to the ground, just in front of Essa, using her light spell to backtrack the prints. Willow guards the rear.

The tracks continue along the cramped tunnel for about fifty yards or so. In Essa's magical light, you see an intersection just ahead where the passage branches sharply to the right and left. The left corridor contains many prints, leading in both directions, including some that enter the tunnel you've just been down. To the right, a lesser number of prints vanish into the darkness, but none return to the intersection.

"It looks like the left trail has been used more than the right one," Kegan says in a hushed voice. "A lot of the prints lead into this tunnel, then on into the zombie chamber."

"Kegan's right," you tell the others. "And the tracks are more widely spaced here. It looks as though whatever made them was running."

"And none of them turned to the right, either," Kegan adds. "They all went to the left, as if they knew just where to go!"

"Out!" the kender snorts huskily. "Where they came from! And that's where we're going!" Willow pushes past all of you and takes several steps into the left branch of the tunnel.

"Wait!" calls Essa quickly. The elf's soft voice is tinged with an unusual degree of excitement, surprising enough to stop the impetuous kender. "The tracks to the right don't return, while some of those to the left do. Perhaps those fleeing the zombies were forced to retrace their steps to this spot, then found their way out of the Sla-Mori to the right."

"Well, Ranger?" Willow asks impatiently. "Is she right? Which prints were made first—the running ones or the walking ones? Which way should we take?"

You bend closer to the jumble of footprints in the dust of the intersection, trying to read their message.

If you decide the way out of the Sla-Mori is to the right, turn to **84**. If you decide that the way out is to the left, turn to **125**.

60

Hurling the scrolls aside, you draw Fireborn and prepare to fight the dragonmen. Three of them fan out around you, driving you away from Willow and Kegan, while the other four monsters block the doorway. Willow has her kender hoopak raised, waiting for a chance to fling its deadly missiles at the draconians, while your brother is standing bravely at her side with the long carving knife raised like a shortsword. You shout a loud battle cry and lunge at the nearest draconian.

Roll two dice to hit and add their total to your fighting skill score. If the result is 12 or more, turn to **12**. If it is less than 12, subtract 4 hit points and turn to **189**. If you feel you are losing, you may choose to surrender (turn to **51**) or to try to escape (turn to **12**) at any point in the action.

61

Essa points to the floor of the corridor at the hideous decayed feet of the zombies and screams an intense phrase. A stream of fire streaks from her fingertips, drawing a flaming line from wall to wall on the dingy floor. The sorceress raises her hand, holding her arm perfectly rigid. The fiery line suddenly bursts into a great wall of flame, forming a barrier of searing heat between the undead monsters and your party.

The heat is so intense that you're forced to shield your face with your arms and back away into the cooler recesses of the narrow passageway. Essa remains welded to the same spot, her soft yellow leather garments beginning to smoke from the ovenlike heat. Her face and eyes glow wildly in the light of the magical fire. Then her taut body suddenly goes limp, and she sags against the rock wall, then catches herself and turns quickly.

"We must leave before the wall of flame dies. The zombies won't cross it, and I doubt if they'll follow us if we're out of sight when it vanishes."

It's obvious to you that the elven sorceress is

greatly weakened by the powerful spell, and you support her as you follow Kegan and Willow along the rocky tunnel. Behind you, the barrier of flames dims just as you dodge around a sharp turn in the narrow passage.

"We're safe now," Essa says, her voice already a bit stronger than a few moments before. You notice for the first time that her spell light is not as bright, sapped by the tremendous effort she used to create the wall of flame. As the light gradually returns to its full brightness, you examine this new corridor, using your Ranger skills to study every small track in the dust of the floor. Turn to **59**.

62

While the hobgoblins' pikes are lowered, you leap at them, drawing Fireborn and slashing furiously at the same time!

Roll two dice to hit and add the result to your fighting skill score. If the total is 11 or more, turn to **197**. If it is less than 11, subtract 3 hit points and turn to **189**. If you think you are in danger of losing at any point, you may choose to surrender (turn to **51**) or to retreat (turn to **172**).

63

"My name is Willow. Willow Lighthand. And you're Bern Vallenshield, the famous Ranger of Crystalmir valley, according to Kegan. He's asleep, over there in the corner. Don't wake him. He's told me all about you!" She giggles.

"I can imagine!" you growl irritably. Closing your eyes, you hope the kender will take the hint and be quiet, even as you realize that it's useless. Kenders are insatiably curious and love to talk. Most people try to use intimidation to protect themselves against

66

kender curiosity, but kenders are totally immune to the emotion of fear, so such threats are meaningless. The best way to handle them, you recall, is by being as nosy as they are.

"If you must talk," you say with a sigh, "tell me about yourself. Where're you from? You're not from Solace. The only kender I know from the Solace is named Burrfoot—Tasselhoff Burrfoot."

"You know Uncle Tas!" Willow exclaims brightly. "Then maybe you know where he's gone off to. I came looking for him. I figured if anyone knew where an adventure was, Uncle Tas would know."

"Well, you're right there," you say. "He and those strange friends of his hadn't been in town thirty minutes before they got mixed up with a barbarian woman and a blue crystal staff. They threw Hederick, the High Theocrat, headfirst into the fire pit in the Inn of the Last Home, killed some of the Fewmaster's guards, and escaped in a stolen boat. At least that's the story I heard."

"Wow!" Willow says, her eyes shining. Then her face falls. "And I missed it," she says sadly. Then she cheers up again. "But it looks as if I've gotten involved in my own adventure!" she adds.

"Mmmmm." You shift position, trying to get comfortable. You note with some envy that your brother is still sleeping peacefully, and you wish this kender girl would leave you alone. Kenders have a habit of getting into trouble and you're in enough trouble already! Still, you do need information. But there's no telling where it will lead you! Even then, you may not be able to believe what you find out.

If you decide to break off this conversation with the kender girl, turn to **26**. But if you choose to keep talking, even though you feel you'll probably regret this new friendship, turn to **137**.

64

"If we try to hide in the women's cell, Verminaard and his henchmen would probably hold them responsible for hiding us," you tell the kender. "I've seen how hobgoblins torture women, and it isn't very pretty. The guardroom's out, for obvious reasons, so I guess we're left with the gully dwarves."

"Perhaps you're right," answers Willow, "but I just don't trust those filthy gully dwarves."

The girl leads you away from the landing as the voices of the guards become louder. Soon they will have searched the upper level and will know that you've come to the cellar. The corridor runs straight to a closed door, where it turns sharply to the right.

"This is the guardroom, and the women's cells are inside," says Willow in a husky whisper. Turn to **35**.

65

You swing Fireborn and manage to nick the griffon's feathered leg just above the talons that hold your waist. The monster shrieks a deafening cry of pain and seizes your sword arm in its gigantic beak. Your mind reels with horror when you realize that the numbness that suddenly replaces the pain is caused by severed nerves! Just before you faint from loss of blood, you glimpse your father's legacy of volcanic steel plunging to the ground below as the griffon swallows your arm in one monstrous gulp.

You try to control your emotions as Willow suggests, but against your will, a feeling of horror begins
as a tiny spark deep in your brain and spreads rapidly. Your palms begin to sweat profusely, and you
can feel your heart pounding like a drum inside your
chest. The only thing you can feel is an irrational,
uncontrollable fear.

"Bern!" shouts Willow. "It's only a spell! You can
fight it if you try!"

But the kender's voice comes too late. You shrink
away from her and Kegan, fearing even your younger brother. You can do nothing except cower in the
dark corner of Flamestrike's chamber until a squad
of hobgoblins come to lead you in chains back to the
quarries of Pax Tharkas.

Fireborn's legendary blade of volcanic steel strikes
the monster's chitinous head, splattering your legs
with its oily juices. The carrion crawler lurches to
one side against the timbered frame of the crypt, and
you leap to one side to avoid its crushing weight.
Finally the huge insect collapses, its tentacles jerking spasmodically in the light of Essa's spell. Willow
rushes to examine the dead creature, controlled once
more by her insatiable kender curiosity.

"Be careful!" you whisper. "It may only be
stunned!"

"Hah! Anything with a gash like that in its noggin
is more than just stunned, Ranger!" she exclaims.
"I'm surprised that a mere human like you could
strike such a blow. Good job, Bern!"

You may now borrow Willow's talisman to heal
some of your wounds. Roll one die and add the result
to your hit points, then turn to **162**.

68

"Are you absolutely sure you don't have kender blood in your family somewhere?" she giggles. "Sometimes you sound just like my brothers!"

"I'm sure. Now drop it," you say indignantly. Then, to your horror, you see Willow begin to open and close drawers, picking things up occasionally to examine them, then absentmindedly dropping the more interesting knickknacks in one of her pockets.

"What in the world are you doing?" you cry angrily. "Aren't we in enough trouble already? You can't steal from the Dragon Highlord!"

"Steal?" Willow's eyes look hurt. "I'm not stealing anything."

"Then what's this?" Grimly you reach into Willow's pocket and pull out a small ivory elephant.

"Hmm," she says, blinking. "How did that get in there? It must have just fallen inside when I wasn't looking."

"Just leave everything alone!" you insist, looking around.

The Dragon Highlord's quarters are a suite of three adjoining rooms, each connected by locked vallenwood doors with polished brass fixtures. The outer chamber seems to be a waiting room, filled with plush furnishings unlike the marred splendor elsewhere in Pax Tharkas. Several lighted candelabra illuminate the formal room with a rich, soft light. An excellent tapestry embroidered with a scene of a rampaging red dragon destroying a village hangs on the rear wall, and a crystal wine set with matching goblets and decanter adorns a small polished table.

"There doesn't seem to be much here anyway," Willow says in hurt tones. "But there might be something in this room."

"That door's probably locked!" you say. "Leave it alone!"

"Oh, Bern, don't be such a stick-in-the-mud." Willow glares at you as she pulls out a long piece of thin wire and reaches for the door.

If you think you're in enough trouble already and you try to stop her, turn to **38**. If you think you might learn something in the locked room and you decide to risk it, turn to **103**.

69

Strange-looking creatures, the like of which you've never seen on Krynn before, work side by side with hobgoblin guards, dragging women and children from the blacksmith shop and keeping the men under watchful guard. They herd all of them into huge carts that look like prison cells on wheels. The strange creatures have the faces and bodies of reptiles, but they walk upright and handle weapons like men! You also notice small leathery wings sprouting from their backs, and you decide they must be the draconians Cleva mentioned! You begin to believe her story about dragons after all!

At that moment, Theros, the giant smithy, comes out of the shop, guarded by two draconians. You see a look of hatred on his dusky face, and his huge fists clench in anger at the way the dragonmen treat the village women, but he is helpless to do anything.

Even as you watch, you see the dragonmen force the smithy back to work, repairing their weapons and their armor. Suddenly a familiar shrill voice twists like a knife in your brain. You see Kegan struggling in the grasp of a large creature dressed in steel armor. Beneath the horned helmet, you recognize the flat, cruel face of a hobgoblin officer. The burly monster is carrying your brother toward the road to join the other captives, and it'll have to pass within a few feet of your hiding place!

If you decide to attack the hobgoblin, turn to **79**. If you prefer to remain hidden until you have a better opportunity to rescue your brother and the other hostages, turn to **14**.

70

You barely have time to draw Fireborn before the draconians burst through the doorway. In the white glow of Essa's light spell, their leathery wings and shining armor fill the cramped space, backing you all against the crates and debris of the cellar. Willow, always the fearless kender, raises her hoopak with a deadly stone aimed at the nearest draconian.

"Stop, Willow!" you shout. "There's a whole army of them on the other side of the door! If we fight them, we'll all be killed! We've got to stay alive in order to have any chance at all of stopping Verminaard."

"Listen to Bern! His words are wise," says Essa. "Go with them now and wait for me to free you!"

You turn to ask the beautiful mage what she means, but her lithe elven body seems to be dissolving into thin air, her enchanted light replaced by the harsher yellow glow of the draconian torches. The monsters swarm around you, jerking Fireborn from your hand and Willow's hoopak from hers. Kegan, standing between the two of you with the butcher's knife, looks confused, but finally he tosses it on the cellar floor just before the draconians push you through the door out into the lighted guardroom.

Your only chance now is to stay alive in the slave pits of Pax Tharkas, nurtured by the hope that the beautiful elven sorceress will be able to counteract Verminaard's evil powers and rescue you somehow.

71

With a final burst of light, the medallion begins to fade, until you feel only the touch of cold metal on your skin. You notice with a start that the pain in your head is gone, and even the gash is healed!

"Are you some kind of a witch? Or a cleric?" you whisper quietly.

"Of course not!" Willow replies. "Kender folks don't study magic. Uncle Tas is the only person I've ever known who talks about clerics. Until now, I thought this medallion was just a pretty piece of jewelry. Believe me, I'm as surprised as you are."

"It must be some kind of healing talisman," you say thoughtfully. "Let's keep it handy. I have a feeling this may be just the kind of thing we'll need at Pax Tharkas!" Turn to **133**.

72

"Help! Stop the slave!"

Behind you, the old hobgoblin is yelling to the guards in the smelter cave. Ignoring them, you race for the boulders on the slope. As you near the slope, you see a squad of armed goblins emerging from the cave. You turn away and run toward the larger cave, hoping that the heavily armored monsters will not be able to catch you. Turn to **128**.

73

You catch sight of a glow out of the corner of your eye, and it gives you an idea. "Willow's necklace!" you exclaim suddenly. "If it has healing powers, it might have other clerical powers. And I've heard stories that the ancient clerics could turn zombies!"

The crystal medallion on the kender's chest is blazing now with a multicolored glare. As its rays dance across the decayed faces, they begin to have a strange effect. The creatures suddenly stop in their tracks, as if they fear the light of the medallion.

"Willow's necklace is stopping them!" you shout.

"You're right, Bern! It must be a cleric's stone of some kind!" gasps Essa. "I, too, have read of such talismans that can be used against the undead."

"Let's get out of here while we've got the chance!" you say, your voice shaking. Willow walks slowly down the corridor, closely followed by you, Essa, and Kegan. The zombies stand aside, letting you pass. Turn to **50**.

74

On the morning of your third day at Pax Tharkas, you spot the large hobgoblin who commanded the goblins at the forge in Solace. The burly officer is eating in the kitchen, obviously still drunk from the night before. Its helmet lies on the table beside it, and its filthy hair dangles in the plate of food before it.

The monster is either too drunk or too sleepy to recognize you. You can hear the gully dwarf cooks mumbling among themselves about having to feed people at all hours, but the hobgoblin can only stare at the angry dwarves with glassy eyes. Suddenly the officer's hairy face droops, then crashes into the bowl of leftover stew in front of it.

The gully dwarves laugh loudly. Then, before you realize what is happening, the filthy little creatures are swarming all over the unconscious hobgoblin, pulling out its money purse and any other valuables they can find.

As the hobgoblin's unconscious form topples from its chair onto the floor with a thud, you nearly cry out with surprise. Protruding from the officer's scabbard, amid the rolls of its unarmored fat belly, you see the familiar hilt of your sword, Fireborn! You're determined to get your sword back, but will you have to fight off these gully dwarves to do it? They look like cowards, but you can't really be sure.

If you decide to attack the gully dwarves to get your sword, turn to **152**. But if you'd rather try to outwit the gully dwarves, turn to **135**.

75

You waste no time examining the corpses of the two dogs. You know you must free the warriors before their masters find the dogs' mangled corpses. You return to the door of the prison wagon and try once more to force the lock open with your dagger.

"Look out, Bern! Behind you!"

The warning from someone inside the wagon almost comes too late. You fling your body aside just as the heavy iron ball and chain of a battle-flail smashes into the bars of the door where your head had been only an instant before. You twist your head around to stare directly into the reptilian eyes of one of the dragonmen!

The short, powerful creature jerks its flail from the door and starts toward you, its thin black tongue slithering forward like a snake's.

You prepare to meet its charge, with your dagger in one hand and Fireborn in the other. Roll two dice to hit and add your fighting skill score to the total. If the result is 12 or more, turn to **29**. If it is less than 12, subtract 4 hit points, then turn to **53**.

However, if you have less than 20 hit points, you don't have enough strength to fight and must surrender. Turn to **117**. If you have 20 or more hit points, you can choose to make a run for it if you wish. Turn to **107**.

Despite your combined efforts, the heavy doors refuse to budge.

"We may be able to escape through the outer door of the other tower," Willow suggests. "It opens into a large prison where several hundred women are held."

"It's worth a try—especially since our choices are limited at this point," you agree. "Lead the way."

The kender girl cracks open the playroom door and steps stealthily into the carpeted hall. She darts quickly to the left, where two huge closed doors stand at the end of the hall. By the time you and Kegan reach her side, she has already opened one of them and vanished inside. You follow and find yourself in a huge corridor, nearly a hundred feet wide and perhaps four times as long.

You know this must be the main corridor connecting the twin towers of Pax Tharkas. It opens to the outside through gigantic portals at both the front and the rear of the citadel. The massive slabs of hewn vallenwood extend all the way from the stone floor to the timbered roof. The front and rear main portals of the citadel are barred by the largest beams you've ever seen. It would take a company of strong warriors to even budge one of the bars that guard the entrances to Pax Tharkas.

The three of you stare in wonder at the magnificent corridor as you make your way down it. You try to be quiet, although every footstep seems to echo like thunder in the great empty hall. At its far end, you reach another pair of closed doors, identical to those outside the playroom. Willow motions for you to be quiet, while she opens one of the doors slightly to peer inside. Over her shoulder, you can see an empty entry hall, with a single small door at its far end and large double doors in the center of the right-hand wall. Both doors are shut, but while you are trying to decide what to do, the double doors bang open, and five draconians come into view. Turn to **87**.

77

The fierce expression in Essa's elven eyes disturbs you, but you need this sword!

"I think you should listen to Willow, Essa. There's no way for us to know what may happen before we get out of here. This could very well be our only chance to stop Verminaard."

"Right!" exclaims the kender, turning to grab Wyrmslayer.

A quick shout from Essa rings out in the cavernous tomb of Kith-Kanan. Instant darkness spreads throughout the chamber, and you know Essa has uttered a magical spell word. The blackness is so dense, so thick, that it seems to suffocate you. You grab for the sorceress, hoping to force her to restore her magical light to the tomb, but she is no longer there. To your left, you can hear Kegan whimpering as the courageous youngster begins to respond as a child to the fears of the Sla-Mori.

"Essa! Restore your light spell!" you demand.

"I cannot," you hear her voice say from somewhere off to your right. "I can summon the aura only once in a day's time. I didn't want to do this, but the tomb of Kith-Kanan must not be violated!"

"That's crazy!" cries Willow's husky voice. The kender's voice sounds as if she has moved closer to Kegan in the darkness, and the boy's whimpering has stopped. "All we are now is food for the rats! We might as well be blind!"

"You forget that I can still see," says the beautiful mage. "The heat from your bodies makes you visible to my elven eyes. I shall lead you out of the Sla-Mori if you will step exactly where I tell you."

"Why should we trust you after this?" demands Willow.

"Because you have no choice," answers the sorceress. "It is I who cannot trust you to respect the sacred relics of Kith-Kanan! Move three paces to your right, kender. Take the boy with you."

"Do as she says," you call to Willow. "We have to trust her now!"

You hear the sound of slow footsteps approaching your side, and you realize that Essa has directed Willow to join you. When her footsteps stop, you hold out your hand.

"Grab my hand, Willow!" you tell the kender. When you feel the girl's warm palm against yours, you pull her gently against your chest and feel Kegan's arm held tightly in her other hand.

"What now, Essa?" you ask.

"Turn slowly and come straight toward my voice," orders the elf from somewhere behind you. You do as she says and continue to obey her directions until you feel yourself entering a passageway of some kind. "Touch the wall on your right and keep on walking," comes Essa's voice once more. "Whatever you do, do not remove your hand from the wall!"

"For how far?" you ask, but you hear no reply.

"Bern! I—I think she's gone!" Kegan murmurs worriedly.

"But not far, I'll wager!" says Willow, her hand squeezing yours in anger. "I wish I could get my hands on those pointed ears of hers!"

"Be quiet, both of you!" you tell them. "Can't you see that she's trying to help us? Let's just follow this wall and see where it leads."

The corridor twists and turns in the inky blackness for what seems like an eternity before you see a dim light of some kind directly ahead. You lead the others forward cautiously until you see a thin line of light along the wall where the tunnel ends. It seems to be a secret door!

"You will find yourself in a valley below Pax Tharkas," you hear Essa's voice call from the darkness. Somehow she has gotten behind you now. "There are resistance fighters against Verminaard's evil forces living in the hills. Ask for a man named Eben Shatterstone. I know nothing of him, but I know he is their leader."

"But what about you?" you cry, suddenly wishing you had not listened to Willow back in the tomb of Kith-Kanan.

"I must return to my homeland with word of what I have discovered."

"But won't the journey be dangerous?" you cry. "We'll go with you."

"No, Bern. I dare not trust you, and only those we trust are allowed into Qualinesti. Farewell, Bern. It seemed for a brief time that my people were wrong and that I had found a human whom I could trust as much as a Qualinesti brother, but it was I who was wrong. Go now, so that you will be able to reach the forest before nightfall."

In the dim light from the crack under the door, you

see a sudden flash of light reflecting off something, and you hear Essa utter something in the elven tongue. Suddenly the door slides open!

The three of you pass through the secret entrance to the Sla-Mori and find yourselves standing in a niche in the base of a sheer granite cliff directly beneath the twin towers of Pax Tharkas. The secret door to Kith-Kanan's tomb closes behind you silently, and you know it would be useless to try to enter again.

Essa's disappointment with you is painful, but for now, all that you can do is take Willow and Kegan far away from Pax Tharkas. Silently you vow to find this Eben Shatterstone and join his resistance fighters. At least, you'll still have some chance to rid the land of the evil Verminaard.

You have emerged from the dreaded Sla-Mori, and Pax Tharkas, alive. Next time you play this adventure, you may credit yourself with one extra experience point.

78

During the next several days, you learn more about the iron mines and the citadel. You also find yourself regaining your strength.

As "punishment" for your "insolent" behavior, you're forced to work with the gully dwarves in the kitchens of Pax Tharkas, where you spend your days scrubbing huge pots and pans used by the gully dwarf cooks and doing other menial tasks. At first you thought you were getting off easy, but after only a few hours, you decided you'd give anything to be slaving away in the mines!

The gully dwarves, as Willow warned you, are truly disgusting creatures. The only edible food they cook goes to feed Lord Verminaard. The stew that is cooked for everyone else contains whatever they can scrounge up to dump in it. You've seen them throw in everything from live rats to dead lizards. Your appetite fades immediately, and you realize that you'll probably starve to death if you have to stay here very long. What amazes you is that the gully dwarves themselves seem to thrive under these conditions and consider their foul stew a work of culinary art!

You're expected to help in the kitchen from dawn until night, when, exhausted, you are finally allowed to return to your cell and eat your foul supper, after which you must return the pots and dishes to the kitchen and wash them. Sometimes it's midnight before you're allowed to stumble back to your cell to get what sleep you can before you are awakened once more at dawn. Roll one die for healing, add the total to your hit points, then turn to **74**.

79

You bound from behind the trees and rush the hobgoblin, who carries Kegan's struggling body under one arm. The monster's face twists in surprise as it shouts a quick command in the goblin language.

A squad of four goblins rush to their commander's aid as their leader hoists Kegan in front of its armored body as a living shield. The goblins are armed with steel shortswords and spears tipped with the same rare metal. They form a bristling semicircle around you, poking the air in front of them with their spears to drive you away from their leader. You tighten your grip on the hilt of Fireborn and swing it at the nearest monster.

Roll two dice to hit, then add your fighting skill score to the sum of the dice. If the grand total is 10 or more, turn to **188**. If the total is less than 10, subtract 2 hit points from your total hit points and turn to **91**.

Remember that you may try to hit the goblin more than once, as long as you subtract 2 hit points each time you miss. Also remember that you may spend experience points to increase your chance at any time as long as you decide how many you are spending before the dice roll and subtract them from your total experience points after you use them.

80

As he hurries past the kitchen counter, you see Kegan grab a large carving knife and thrust it into his belt. You grin at the boy's courage, then urge him forward with a shove.

When you enter the playroom at the other end of the tunnel, you study the double doors leading to the field behind the citadel, wondering if you can force the doors open despite the heavy bars on the outside. You recall that the iron rungs that hold the wooden beams looked rusty. Perhaps the three of you might have a chance to force the doors open.

"Where do those other doors in the hall lead to?" you ask Willow, remembering the other passageway leading from the kitchen.

"To the corridor that connects the two towers," says the kender. "That's the way they marched us into the fortress when they brought us here."

If you decide to try to force open the double doors that lead outside the fortress, turn to **2**. If you choose to enter the hallway leading to the Dragon Highlord's quarters and to the kitchen, turn to **121**. But if you want to cross over to the other tower, turn to **76**.

81

You see some of the Fewmaster's horses tethered in the yard near the blacksmith shop. That gives you an idea. Keeping an eye on the draconian guards lounging in the shade of the smithy's porch, you sneak out of the woods and creep over near the forge.

"Theros!" you call softly, timing it in between the smith's clanging hammer blows.

The big man raises his head, sees you, glances at the guards, then continues his work as if he had heard nothing. But you see him nod slightly to let you know he is listening.

"I need a horse!" you whisper. "Can you give me some cover?"

The smith grins. "Take that dapple mare over there. Good luck, Bern!" he mutters. Lifting the hunk of molten metal he has been working on, the smith takes it up in his tongs and suddenly plunges the red hot metal into a bucket of water near the forge. There is a sharp hiss, and clouds of steam rise from the water. Quickly you slip through the fence, grab the horse's reins, mount it, and ride for your very life!

By the time the draconians realize what is happening, it's too late to stop you. You gallop out of the ravaged town, following the tracks of the prison wagons as darkness begins to fall.

It doesn't take long to catch up with them. But now that they're in sight, what are you going to do? You want to rescue your brother and the other hostages, but that's not going to help you combat whatever evil forces have destroyed Solace!

If you decide to try to rescue your brother, turn to **6**. But if you choose to wait and see if you can learn more about these invaders, turn to **23**.

82

The goblins and draconians snarl commands in Common to the captives as they prod them toward the wagons with their spears. Just as they start to pack them all into the wagons, a shout from the road stops them. You see a stubby figure astride a horse riding quickly toward the caravan. As the figure grows closer, you recognize the loathsome face of Fewmaster Toede, the hobgoblin commandant of the goblins. Toede first appeared in Solace only a few weeks ago, swaggering around town with Hederick, the High Theocrat, demanding to know the location of a mysterious staff of blue crystal.

The Fewmaster looks over the prisoners, and his fat face splits in an evil grin. "Lord Verminaard will be pleased with this lot, eh, Theros?" he calls out to the smithy, who is working at the forge, a huge hammer in his hand.

Theros Ironfeld turns around abruptly. "Someday you and this Lord Verminaard will pay for what you've done to Solace!" he growls, taking a threatening step forward.

Toede blanches and backs his horse up. "Stop him!" he croaks, and two draconians move between the smithy and the Fewmaster. Theros scowls and returns to his work.

Toede gulps and mutters some unintelligible commands in the guttural dialect of goblins. You watch the goblin guards lead many huge elk forward and hitch them to the prison carts. Goblins climb up to the driver's seats, and a few draconian soldiers fall in behind them. You notice, though, that most of the draconians apparently plan to stay in Solace. Toede yells to the lead teamster, whose bullwhip snakes forward, cracking just over the ears of the lead elk. The wagons lurch forward amid the screams of despair from the women and children.

The Fewmaster watches the wagons rumble away behind a cloud of yellow dust before spurring

85

his horse in the opposite direction. As both dust clouds settle, you step from behind the well and try to make some sense of the strange and terrible events that have happened so quickly in your previously quiet village of Solace. Turn to **33**.

83

"We've got to try to rescue the others," you say urgently. "There's no way to know whether we'll ever be able to find help."

You, Kegan, and Willow creep across the courtyard, heading toward the slave mines. Your spirits are high. It shouldn't be too difficult, you think, to get your friends to rise up in rebellion and overthrow their hated guards.

Suddenly, however, you hear what sounds like footsteps behind you. You come to a halt, and Kegan and Willow stop right behind you.

"What's the mat—" Kegan starts to say, but his words change to a gurgle as a huge hobgoblin grabs him around the throat.

You leap forward, but the monster has the advantage of surprise because you weren't paying attention. Turn to **189**.

84

"On close examination, I think the tracks are just too jumbled to tell which ones were made first," you tell the others. "The trail to the right is the only clear set of footprints, and there aren't any signs of a struggle there. If we don't find a way out to the right, we can always retrace our steps and try again."

The kender tosses her coppery pigtails impatiently. "I guess one way's as good as another. One thing's sure. We can't split up because we all need Essa's light spell. Lead on, Ranger!"

Using the elf's magical aura to follow the faint prints in the dust, you track them nearly a hundred yards until the corridor widens into a huge chamber. The light from Essa's spell casts eerie shadows into the depths of the underground hall, spilling over the shapes of tall columns similar to those of the chamber guarded by the zombies. Some of the columns lie broken on the dusty floor, but most of them are still intact, supporting the graceful arches of an ancient ceiling.

Along the wall directly in front of you, you see a magnificent granite throne flanked by two gigantic statues carved of the same material. They are guardians of stone, elven warriors armed with drawn granite broadswords. But your attention is drawn to, not the monstrous statues, but the mummified figure seated on the massive throne between them. Turn to **198**.

85

Before the dragonmen can recover from their surprise, you've already slain two of them, lopping off their heads so that your sword will not remain frozen in their stony bodies. Willow uses her hoopak with deadly accuracy, raining stone missiles on the other draconians and keeping them from joining their comrades against you.

One of the draconians, hit by a glancing blow by one of Willow's missiles, falls to the floor and clutches with one clawed hand for Kegan's ankle. With both hands, your brother plunges his sharp carving knife into the creature's back, killing it instantly, but the knife freezes in the dragonman's corpse.

You leap across the room to your brother's aid, but it isn't necessary. The remaining dragonmen back away through the door to the right, screaming an alarm in their hissing language. Kegan grabs his improvised but deadly weapon as the draconian's corpse crumbles into a pile of stone powder.

"Our only chance is the other tower!" you cry, pushing your younger brother toward the outer door, into the great hall between the twin towers. Willow pauses long enough to lock the heavy door from the outside.

"Handler skills are double-edged," says the kender with a grin. "A door can be unpicked as well as picked!" Turn to **119**.

86

You feel weak from pain and loss of blood. More goblins are rushing in to join in the attack, and you know it would be suicidal to continue fighting. You won't help your brother by getting killed!

"Stop!" you shout, dropping Fireborn to your side. "I surrender. Take me along with my brother—the boy your commander captured." Turn to **45**.

87

The dragonmen are talking loudly in their hissing language, laughing in response to some crude joke. They wear battle-stained scale armor tunics instead of the studded leather of the two dragonmen on the slave caravan from Solace, and you notice that they're armed with shortswords. They pause in the entry hall while one of them finishes a droll story, giving you a few more moments to decide what to do.

If you decide to fight the draconians, turn to **185**. If you think it would be smarter to retreat back to the first tower, turn to **165**.

88

The sinister undead figures begin to stalk toward you. Their armor covers the mummified flesh of their arms and legs, and the reek of their decayed bodies overwhelms your horrified senses. Before you can react, Essa steps in front of you with her palms extended out in front of her, toward the zombies. The graceful sorceress murmurs a low spell word in the elven language. Almost immediately, twin jets of flame swirl in the rancid air between you and the monsters. The flames form into fiery balls, which rocket into the first rank of zombies.

Even as five of the undead creatures collapse in the powerful blast of Essa's magical fireballs, more of the gruesome things stumble relentlessly over the burning corpses. Essa has already drawn the enchanted silver sword, and its magical glow is so strong that it makes the elven sorceress's silver aura seem dim in comparison.

"Essa!" you scream. "Get back! You can't fight them all!" You lunge forward with Fireborn drawn, but a trio of the zombies lumber between you and the beautiful mage.

"Move out of the way, Bern!" yells Willow.

The kender girl is whirling her hoopak sling above her head, trying to get an open shot at the monsters. You shift quickly to one side, slicing at the nearest zombie. Just as Fireborn's blade bites into the undead creature's side, the corridor is plunged into

89

darkness! The zombies have swamped the valiant elven sorceress, extinguishing both her spell light and the aura of her magic sword!

Cries from Willow and Kegan flood your ears, but you can see nothing at all in the thick darkness of Kith-Kanan's tomb. You swing Fireborn desperately in the direction of the last zombies you saw. The sickening stench of rotted flesh is all around you as the steel blade hacks through bloodless corpses and ancient bones. You try to listen for sounds to direct your blows, but the zombies are silent, swarming things. Clawlike fingers rake you, twisting you around until the monsters' horrible bodies press you to the floor in the blackness beneath Pax Tharkas.

89

"You two!" the hobgoblin leader cries to the two draconians guarding the smithy. "After him!"

"The fighter's your problem, not ours," one of the dragonmen replies coldly. "We have orders to stay with the smith."

While they are arguing, you see Theros make a quick gesture with his head. It looks like he's trying to signal you. You decide to sneak to the smith's yard to find out what he's trying to tell you.

Roll to see if you succeed. Roll one die and add the result to your observation skill score. If this total is 6 or more, turn to **81**. If it is less than 6, you failed, were struck over the head, and captured. Roll one die for damage and deduct the result from your hit points, then turn to **114**.

90

Cautiously you creep down the hallway, hoping the small cluster of laughing guards in front of Verminaard's throne room don't notice you. Swiftly you round the corner and head for the room at the end of the hall where the double doors are located. Meeting no one, your heart beats with hope. You enter the empty room and hurry over to the doors. Then your heart sinks. A huge iron bar is across them, apparently to lock the fortress securely for the night.

Roll one die to determine if you can move the bar. Add the result to your physical prowess skill score. If the total is 8 or more, you are successful. Turn to **22**. If it is less than 8, turn to **176**.

91

The goblin blocks your swing with its spear. Other goblins leap at you now, shouting and cursing in anger. One of them strikes you on the head with the butt of its spear. Your head rings and blood flows freely down your face as you stagger backward. "He's young and strong. He'll bring a high price! Take him alive!" the hobgoblin leader shouts as it holds onto Kegan.

"Run, Bern!" your brother shouts. "They're taking us to the slave mines!"

Roll one die for damage and subtract the total from your hit points. If you have less than 28 hit points remaining, you must surrender. Turn to **86**. If you have 28 hit points or more, you have enough strength left to escape. Turn to **104**.

"Stifle that kender curiosity of yours, Willow," you mutter. "The only thing in that direction is Pax Tharkas, and we're not going back there. Of course, if *you* want to know that badly. . . ."

"There are legends of a great chain that ties Pax Tharkas to the ground to keep it from floating away," says Willow in excitement. "Maybe this is it!"

"No kender tales, please!" Essa says. "What Bern says is true. We should be searching for a way out of here, and we might as well start with the other door."

"Okay," Willow says, and before you can stop her, the adventuresome kender has dashed across the room to the bronze portal opposite you.

"Not so fast, Willow!" you call. "You'll outrun Essa's light!"

"Follow the kender," the elven sorceress says, pushing past you to join Willow. When you finally succeed in pulling Kegan away from his fascination with the chain and follow Willow and Essa through the door, you see the mage's magical light vanishing around a turn in a long corridor. You follow them through several such turns until the corridor ends abruptly at a stone wall. Willow and Essa are examining the corners of the wall for signs of an opening.

"It's another dead end!" the kender wails as you approach.

"Maybe not," you say hopefully. "Let's check it out like we did before!"

Roll one die to find the secret door. Add your observation skill points to the result. If the total is 5 or more, turn to **32**. If it is less than 5, turn to **20**.

The smoke nearly suffocates you by the time you climb onto Watchman's Ledge and look down upon the ruined, blackened vale. You wonder what terrible catastrophe could have struck since you left only two days ago. No storm, no matter how severe, has ever done more than stir the branches of the great trees. Even the Cataclysm—when the gods dropped a fiery mountain down upon the world of Krynn—merely forced the natives of Solace to move their homes into the trees. Yet now, everywhere you look, the great trees are nothing but smoldering skeletons. Here and there you spot the remnants of the ancient treehouses that once sheltered the residents of Solace.

"Bern! Bern Vallenshield!"

A hoarse cry startles your confused mind. You crouch in a fighting stance and grasp the solid hilt of Fireborn, your father's legendary steel sword. "Get off the road, Bern! They'll see you! Come and hide in the forest!"

If you think that the voice might be some sort of trap, turn to **58**. But if you feel the stranger's warning might well make sense, turn to **130**.

94

They're the largest hobgoblins you've ever seen, with yellowish skin and gleaming ivory horns on their helmets. Both are armed with polished pikes and wear full suits of chain mail. They turn their heads as you enter the wide corridor and glance at each other questioningly, but they remain at their posts.

"That's Verminaard's council chamber and throne room," Willow whispers. "His private quarters are just beyond those guards."

"Why didn't you tell me he had guards posted?" you demand.

"You didn't ask me," she says lightly, as if it were a

simple matter. "You've already handled a red dragon fairly well, so I thought a hobgoblin or two wouldn't present any problem."

You glare at the kender's innocent smile, wishing that you were somewhere else where you could yell at her.

"Come on, Ranger!" she mutters, rubbing salt into the wound. "How do we handle these ugly creatures?"

You know that, even with Fireborn, you're no match for the two gigantic guards. Besides, in no time, they'd have every draconian in the place after you. You consider your other choices.

If you want to avoid facing the two hobgoblin guards by going downstairs, turn to **131**. If you'd rather try bluffing your way past the guards, turn to **141**.

95

"If the entrance to the Sla-Mori is here, we can't find it!" you exclaim, glancing nervously at the door to the guardroom. The glimmering line around its edge appears fainter now, and the panel is beginning to shake with the pounding of the dragonmen on the other side.

"It has to be here!" cries Essa. "I know it! Please keep looking!"

"It's too late, Essa," Willow says coolly. "Your spell has worn off from the door. Here they come!" Turn to **70**.

The dark figure is one of the dragonmen. It is dressed in a tunic of studded leather like that of the dogs, and it is waving a cruel battle-flail of black iron. The spiked iron ball swings from its heavy chain as the draconian's glassy reptilian eyes stare at you, unblinking. Turn to **117**.

The hobgoblin is still lying, comatose, on the floor where you left it. Reluctantly you take your sword off and rebuckle it around the creature's waist. Then, nearly gagging at the awful smell of the creature, you lift it up and drag its arm across your shoulder. It stumbles and belches, leaning against you drunkenly and heavily.

Staggering under the hobgoblin's weight, you stumble down the hall toward Lord Verminaard's quarters, straight for a group of laughing draconian guards you see lingering outside the throne room. Your heart pounds in your throat. If your plan fails, you know you'll probably be thrown into the slave mines and never let out!

The draconians interrupt their conversation to

stare at you and the drunken hobgoblin in disgust.

"Well?" growls one, eyeing you suspiciously.

"Uh, the captain here ordered me to help him to his quarters," you say, swallowing nervously. "Can you let me out of the fortress?"

"It's Captain Grund, the drunken fool," one of the draconians mutters. "I don't know why his lordship puts up with the likes of idiots like him. Almost as stupid as humans, these hobgoblins." The draconian stares at you, sneering, as you struggle to keep your anger under control. "Just dump him in the hall and let him sleep it off."

You were afraid they might say that. "Please, sir!" you exclaim, looking frightened. "If he doesn't wake up in his quarters, he'll skin me alive!"

The draconian hesitates as your heart pounds in your chest. Then it sighs. "Come on, Dorg," it says. "I suppose we'll have to see old Grund to bed or there'll be trouble." You heave a sigh of relief. Grumbling, the two draconians lead you down the hall, into the empty room, and—between them—open the iron bar across the doorway.

"Thanks," you say, panting, your arms nearly breaking under the dead weight of the hobgoblin.

"Don't thank us, human," the draconian snarls. "I'd just as soon see you skinned!"

The door slams shut, leaving you in the courtyard with the drunken hobgoblin. Turn to **138**.

98

"I think we should listen to Essa," you tell the kender girl. "She's studied the legends of the Sla-Mori and understands the ways of her people better than any human or kender could. If we don't find anything beyond the double doors, we can always return to this door again and satisfy that curiosity of yours."

Willow's eyes flash with a flare of temper, but it passes in an instant. "Perhaps you're right, Bern Vallenshield, but I don't think so. In fact, I think we'll be walking right into a trap if we go that way! But I'll go along. You may need every bit of help you can get!"

"Hey, stop arguing!" Kegan complains. "We're not accomplishing anything just standing here!"

You clap your brother on the shoulder. "My thought exactly, Kegan! Come on."

Essa's light spell guides you through the granite columns and across the central space to the corridor leading to the two doors. They're fashioned of the same heavy bronze as the others, but much larger. Instead of bearing an embossed unicorn design, these bear a perfect replica of Pax Tharkas itself, with the twin towers divided evenly between the pair of doors, so that the thin seam separating them runs right through the main door of the central hallway. The ancient artists who sculpted the gold etched such perfect details as individual planks in the shutters.

You step forward and push on the heavy metal doors, expecting them to be locked. Instead, they swing silently inward with your slightest touch, opening onto a very long hallway. The four of you step through the doors, which close softly behind you as if by some invisible hand. The silvery glow of Essa's spell spreads, revealing a straight corridor extending as far as you can see. It's about forty feet wide, and its walls are broken by twin rows of evenly spaced doors, each with an iron ring in its center.

You begin to walk forward slowly, past the strange granite doors, which seem to be guarding some unknown, dreadful secret. When you've gone a few hundred feet, you see that the corridor ends in a wall straight ahead, but you also see a dark tunnel of some kind off to the right. No one has spoken a word since you entered this eerie passage. Even Willow remains silent for once.

"I don't like this place one bit," Kegan whispers timidly. "It reminds me of a graveyard crypt! Those stone rings might be—"

A sudden noise interrupts your brother. You hear a soft rustling sound, and it seems to be coming from behind those very stone doors! Your hand drops to Fireborn's hilt, and Essa draws the gleaming silver sword she made by magic in the women's prison.

"Look at Willow's necklace!" Kegan whispers. You glance at the kender. The crystal medallion has begun to glow, just as it did when she used it to heal your wounds! But you don't have time to question her about the necklace because an ominous sound of sliding stone tears your eyes away from Willow. All along both sides of the wide hallway, the stone slabs are being pushed open from the other side! Turn to **132**.

99
The drunken goblins fall easy prey to the flashing arc of Fireborn. All around you, the men of Solace are hacking and slashing away with fury as they remember the destruction of their town. Just as it seems victory is within your grasp, you catch sight of movement out of the corner of your eye. A familiar figure leaps onto the back of a goblin, trying to strangle it.

"No! Kegan, stop!" you yell. Shoving aside the goblin you're fighting, you rush toward your brother. Suddenly, to your horror, you catch a fleeting glimpse of a huge spiked ball whizzing toward your head as someone yells, "Bern, look out behind you!" Roll one die for damage, subtract the result from your hit points, and turn to **114**.

100

The three of you rush through Verminaard's suite and out the door. Suddenly you remember the two hobgoblins outside the council chamber. The large guards are standing with their pikes ready to challenge you, and you prepare yourself to fight once more. Willow runs past you before you can stop her and motions to the hobgoblins.

"Something terrible just happened!" she cries. "It's the draconians! They just disappeared!"

The two guards look at each other quickly, wondering if they should leave their post to investigate the kender's story.

"One of you go while the other tells Lord Verminaard!" she suggests frantically. "Go!" Turn to **178**.

101

The creature raises the hilt of its sword. You grit your teeth, but you keep your eyes right on the dragonman, determined to show this creature you are not afraid. Then the hilt of the sword slams into your jaw, and pain explodes inside your head. The last you hear, as you lose consciousness, are the two dragonmen gurgling with laughter. Roll one die for damage and subtract the number from your total hit points, then turn to **114.**.

102

Intent on your efforts to find an unopened crypt, you fail to notice that Kegan has remained at the other end of the corridor. Just as you finish your investigation of the first slab, you raise your head just in time to see the boy pulling on one of the doors you haven't passed yet.

"No, Kegan!" you shout. But it's too late. The slab swings open with a dull grating sound, flooding the corridor once more with the horrible stench of decaying flesh. Turn to **16**.

103

Willow's skillful fingers bend a short length of wire she has taken from the hem of her tunic into a picklock. In less than a minute, you hear the click of the lock and follow the kender girl into the next room.

You've entered a formal dining room, dominated by a magnificent table of gleaming ebony wood. A matching buffet with glass doors protecting a collection of fine china and silver stands against the wall, and there's another locked door in the far right corner of the room. In the rich light of a chandelier, you study the lush colors of two more tapestries with the same sinister themes of dragons and their victims.

"Bern! Look here!"

The kender handler is squatting by a small drawer of the buffet, peering at something inside. You and Kegan turn away from the tapestries and join her. Inside the drawer, you see an open chest with three small vials of clear crystal, each containing tiny amounts of colored fluid. You start to reach for the case, but Willow grabs your hand. Turn to **41**.

104

Blood dims your vision, but you slash viciously at the nearest goblin. Fireborn bites deep into its leather-clad arm, and you whirl around to meet the charge of the second goblin. Your blade parries its spear thrust easily, and you manage to dispose of it with a deft thrust of your blade. The two uninjured attackers hesitate, obviously having second thoughts about charging you.

You are rapidly growing weaker, and you realize you can't hold out much longer. Keeping the goblins at bay with your sword, you back into the woods and disappear into the thick shadows.

You hear the hobgoblin leader shout, "After him!"

"You go in after him," one of the goblins mutters.

Injured, sick at heart, and discouraged, you head back for the road, hoping to find Cleva once more. You have no idea what to do next. Turn to **130**, where you have succeeded in finding Cleva once more.

Flamestrike's clouded eyes blink in the sudden light of the open door. Her forked tongue slithers forward, trying to sense the identity of the intruders in her chamber. The great jaws yawn, displaying rows of rotten, yellowed teeth.

"Is there another way out?" you cry.

"Just through the windows, and they're barred shut. Even if they weren't, there's a drop of a couple hundred feet," your brother replies.

"Bern, the only way out is the way we came in!" Willow says excitedly. "Even if we make it back past Flamestrike, the guards will hear the alarm and they'll catch us before we get out of the citadel!"

You realize there is no way you can fight the dragon without endangering the lives of the children. You decide only two options remain. If you decide to stand your ground and try to bluff your way out, turn to **25**. But if you figure you'd better run for it, turn to **7**.

"Where do we start?" Kegan whispers anxiously. "I sure don't want to wake up those zombies again!"

"What if we look for a crypt that hasn't been opened yet?" suggests Willow. "That'll probably mean it's empty, so it might be hiding a secret passage out of this place!"

"I don't like the word 'might,' Willow," says your brother, glancing around the somber corridor at the rows of closed tombs.

"It's a chance we'll just have to take," you tell Kegan. "If we go any farther, we'll have to pass a dozen more of these slabs and face more of the zombies anyway. Let's get busy. Look for a crypt door that looks like it hasn't been disturbed."

The four of you begin to retrace your steps, back toward the double doors opening onto the great columned hall. Each of the stone slabs you check bears signs of recent movement, probably caused when the zombies emerged from their tombs to attack you. Your nerves are raw as you carefully work your way closer to the twin doors, prepared to meet another attack of the undead creatures at any moment. Turn to **52**.

You turn your head and see the large hobgoblin who captured Kegan leading the other guards toward you. You glance at the shadows by the cliff where the dapple mare is waiting patiently and try to estimate how far you could get before the spears cut you down.

Just at that moment, a crushing blow strikes your head and darkness closes around you. Roll one die for damage, subtract the result from your hit points, and turn to **114**.

108

You stare at Willow's calm face, trying to fight the growing pangs of fear deep inside your brain. At first, you doubt that you can ever hope to control the horrible feelings that threaten to take over your mind, but the calmness of the glow fades from Flamestrike's upturned snout, the fear within you begins to subside, and you know that you have won.

"Thank you, Mother, for doing such a good job of protecting your children!" you call to the wretched monster. "I'll be sure to report your great concern for them to the Dragon Highlord. Come on, nestling. We have work to do!"

The wrinkled red snout grins in pride as you lead Kegan, flinching, from the dragon's chamber. From your brother's chagrined expression, you know that he resents being called a nestling. You pass through the kitchen tunnel, hearing only the sounds of Flamestrike's wheezing breathing behind you. Turn to **80**.

109

An overripe melon strikes the wall right where your head had been, splattering all of you with its rancid pulp and juice. Across the large chamber, you see several overturned chairs and dozens of the dirty gully dwarf laborers piled in a twisted heap of flailing fists and kicking feet.

"Don't be alarmed," says Willow. "It's nothing serious—only their daily food fight and free-for-all!"

You start to pick off bits of smelly melon in disgust, when suddenly one of the gully dwarves comes running over to you. As he approaches, you see that his beard is grayer and much longer than that of any of the others.

"Hey, stop that!" he yells, pointing at you. "You want breakfast, you pay!"

"Breakfast?" you say in astonishment.

The gully dwarf points to the melon rind you hold in your hand. "You eat, you pay!" he says, glaring at you.

"I wouldn't eat this fil—" you begin, but Willow punches you in the ribs. You glance at Willow, suddenly wishing you had listened to her when she was doubtful about seeking aid from the gully dwarves. Now she just shrugs her shoulders and grins, as if to say, "I told you so." "Uh, thanks," you say, "but we're not hungry. We're, uh, escaping from the Dragon Highlord, you see, and we need someplace to hide."

The other gully dwarves suddenly stop their food fight and gather around you and Kegan and Willow, apparently deciding you are more entertaining. They poke and prod at you with their filthy hands, while Kegan giggles.

"You no eat?" the gully dwarf asks, surprised. Then, seeing you shake your head, he reaches out and grabs the melon rind. "Then don't waste good food!"

"I'm sorry," you say, trying to keep your frustration under control. Even as you're talking, you can hear the guards searching for you! "What about a place to hide?"

"You hide, you pay," the gully dwarf says, glancing

107

behind him at the others, who nod enthusiastically.

"I don't have mon—" you begin, but again Willow pokes you. Turning, you see the kender emptying various pockets and pouches she wears, spilling all sorts of odd items onto the floor—pieces of string, bits of ribbon, a broken clay horse, three baby teeth, a brass ring. . . .

"Wow!" says the gully dwarf, his eyes wide as he and the others scramble around to pick up the collection of worthless items. "You rich person! You king or something?" he asks Willow.

"No," she giggles. "Just a kender. *Now* will you hide us?"

"You betcha! Over here!" The gully dwarf grabs your hand and drags you across the food-spattered floor over to a pile of filthy blankets. "Lie down on top of blankets," he says. "Good hiding place."

"Uh, don't you think it'd be an even better hiding place if we lie down *under* the blankets?" you ask.

The gully dwarf stares at you with dawning respect. "Hey! You smart!" He turns to the other gully dwarves. "Hide *under* blanket," he repeats and the others nod enthusiastically, genuinely impressed with your genius.

Shaking your head with a sigh, you and Kegan and Willow quickly crawl under the stinking blankets—and not a second too soon. You hear a heavy fist pound on the door, then the sound of the door slamming against the wall.

"We're looking for escaped prisoners—a kender, a human Ranger, and a human kid. You creeps seen them?" asks a gruff voice that you recognize as a hobgoblin's.

"Escaped prisoners?" you hear the gully dwarf say in what he thinks is a tone of innocence. "We no see escaped prisoners," he says. And you hear the other gully dwarves chime in, saying, "No escaped prisoners here."

"Well, all right," the hobgoblin growls. You hear his boots start to shuffle out of the room, and you begin to breathe easier, when suddenly your heart sinks.

"We especially no see escaped prisoners *under* blankets!" adds the gully dwarf solemnly.

110

"Wait!" roars the dragon. "I must prepare him for danger!"

If you elect to stop and try to discover what the awesome nursemaid means, turn to **174**. But if you decide to make a run for it, turn to **7**.

111

The sounds of boisterous laughter tell you that the goblin guards are still enjoying their wine and food. You open the barred door and, one by one, help the captive warriors file silently out of the prison wagon. Just as the last man drops to the ground, you hear a clatter behind you and turn in time to see the stone statue of the draconian's body crumble to dust. Fireborn falls to the ground, along with the draconian's flail, armor, and clothing. You grab both weapons and toss the flail to the nearest warrior.

"Our weapons are under the teamster's seat in the

first wagon!" whispers one of the men. "I saw them load them there before we left Solace!"

You lead the men to the rear of the prison wagon, keeping in the shadows at the foot of the cliff. In single file, you skirt the wagons, listening to the raucous sounds of the drunken goblins. Hastening your steps, you point to the first wagon and move aside to let the silent warriors collect their arms and shields. Then, their weapons in hand, the men fan out beside the darkened caravan. By this time, the goblins have become so unruly with drink that their shouts conceal any small noises made by your men. Several goblins have grabbed their spears and are shaking the steel points at each other.

When all your men are in place, you raise your sword and yell, "Take them, men of Crystalmir! For Solace!" And with Fireborn's flawless blade gleaming in the firelight, you bound into the campsite hacking furiously at the confused goblins.

Roll two dice to determine the outcome of the melee for you and your men. Add your fighting skill score to the total of the dice. If the result is 10 or more, turn to **56**. If it is less than 10, subtract 2 hit points and turn to **99**.

"I think it would be a mistake to follow these rodent tracks," you tell your companions. "In places like this, rats feed by following larger scavengers and eating their leftovers."

"You mean like the carrion crawler?" Kegan asks with a shudder.

"Exactly! We know there are probably more of those things down here, and the rats would know just where they are!"

"And the crawlers wouldn't be far from the zombies!" adds Willow, an excited glimmer in her fearless eyes.

"So that leaves the unmarked tunnel," you tell them. "The rats have probably avoided it because there's nothing down there for them to eat."

"Or because something's there that would eat *them!*" Willow suggests, a twinkle in her eye. You scowl at the kender's sense of humor and motion for Essa to walk behind you so that her spell light can brighten the narrow passage. Turn to **195**.

113

"Stop!" you shout, lowering your sword. "Don't kill him!" One of the creatures grabs Fireborn while another throws you against the stone wall and ties your hands behind your back.

You've made a desperate attempt to end the menace of Verminaard's evil plans for Ansalon, but from now on, someone else will have to fight the Dragon Highlord. . . .

114

The next sensation you feel is one of softness, of warmth, and of movement beneath your body. You open your eyes and see a dark head with long hair silhouetted against the starry sky through the bars of a wagon. You're flat on your back, and your head is lying on something soft. It takes you several moments to realize that your head is resting on a woman's lap.

"Shhh. Don't try to talk," she says in an accent you recall from somewhere. "You've got a nasty wound on your head. You need to rest before we get to Pax Tharkas."

Suddenly you recognize the accent. "You're a kender!" you mumble weakly. You sit up quickly, searching wildly through your leather tunic for your money pouch. "All right! Where is it?" you demand angrily.

The kender girl looks at you in amazement. "I haven't any idea what you're talking about! Boy, that must have been some clout on the head!"

"My money!" you say furiously, then the pain in your head brings a wave of dizziness over you, and you are forced to lie back down—this time with your head on the wooden bench.

"Oh, that!" the girl says. "Well, why didn't you say so? I took it, of course."

"Of course," you groan.

"But only to keep the goblins from finding it when they searched you," the kender girl adds with a hurt expression on her face.

Sure, you think. Everyone in Krynn knows about kenders and their talent for "acquiring" things. And they *never* mean to take them.

"Where—where am I?" you ask weakly.

"In a prison wagon, on the way to Pax Tharkas, Bern," the kender says, handing you your money pouch.

"How do you know my name?" you ask suspiciously. "And just who are you, anyway?"

Turn to **63**.

"Get inside quickly," Essa orders. "I want to make sure no one follows us."

You squeeze through the opening, past the elf, and stop to wait for her to join you. The mage whispers an incantation and tosses some of the cave dust into the air at the mouth of the tunnel. The pinch of dust becomes thicker and floats out of the tunnel into the cellar. It settles over every inch of the floor, covering your tracks so completely that even your trained Ranger's eye can't detect a single sign that you have passed this way. Satisfied that the draconians will never be able to find the hidden door, Essa pulls a lever, sealing you inside the ancient elven catacombs called the Sla-Mori. Turn to **10**.

116

Turning, you see the figure of a man dressed entirely in blue and gold plate mail, bent over some maps spread on top of a long council table. You can't see the Dragon Highlord's face because it is hidden behind a dark metal visor with a grotesque face drawn on it in gold. A pair of painted horns protrude from the top of his helmet, giving you the impression of a dragon.

"Answer me, I say! Ember! Come!" Verminaard shouts impatiently.

Just behind the evil cleric, you hear the sound of something very large, as if it were inside the walls. Before you have time to do anything, a set of huge double doors fly open, revealing the kind of hideous creature you have seen only in your nightmares. It's another red dragon, much like Flamestrike but far more dangerous-looking! The great beast studies the three of you without blinking. Its slithering black tongue glides forward, hovering in the air only inches from your faces.

You glance at Willow and Kegan, only to see that they're standing as motionless as statues, their eyes clouded and dull.

Suddenly there's a pounding at the door. "Lord Verminaard! Are you in there?" demands one of the

Dragon Highlord's private guards, one of the draconians you saw across the hall.

In the instant that Verminaard's attention is diverted by the dragonmen, you know that you can strike—if you dare!

If you decide to attack Lord Verminaard, turn to **177**. But if you reason that this man is too powerful and choose to surrender, turn to **147**.

117

The dragonman begins to circle around you, trying to get between you and the prison wagon, hissing with barely a movement of its scaly lips.

Suddenly you have an idea. If you fight this creature, you may win, but the noise would probably attract the goblins and the other draconian from the campfire, and you may never have a chance to discover who or what was behind the destruction of Solace. But if you surrender, it may be possible to find a way to rescue your brother as well as the other captives. That way, you might also learn more about the mysterious power that burned your home village.

"I came to free my people from these cages! Where are you taking them? Why have you burned Solace to the ground?"

The draconian's laughter is loud enough to be heard at the campfire, and several voices shout in your direction. "You'll know soon enough, Ranger! Look behind you!" Turn to **107**.

118

You have learned something about the layout of the fortress from your own observations in the last few days. You tried questioning the gully dwarves to find out more, but they were even vague about where their own quarters were.

The doors you usually use to get to the kitchen are down the hallway. But the hall has always been dark when you were brought to the kitchen. You have no idea what the rooms you pass by are used for. How will you get out?

You know that Lord Verminaard's quarters are only a few paces down the hallway, and they are always heavily guarded, so you want to stay away from there. But you might be able to sneak past them without being noticed, especially if you looked like you were on an errand. The sight of the drunken hobgoblin gives you an idea, however—a dangerous one!

If you decide to try to sneak out by yourself, turn to **90**. But if you elect to follow through on your idea, turn to **97**.

119

You race for the first tower, your footsteps echoing loudly in the cavernous passage. Behind you, the shouts of the draconians are muffled as they try to batter their way through the heavy panel of vallenwood.

"It won't take them long to get through that door!" you exclaim as you reach the other end of the corridor. "We'll have to hide in the cellar or we'll be caught between the Dragon Highlord's bodyguards and the draconians." Turn to **131**.

120

Tensing your muscles, you jab your elbow into the gut of the dragonman holding your arms behind you. The creature, not expecting you to attack, doubles over in pain. Quickly you draw your sword.

You have gained a momentary advantage. Roll two dice to hit, then add your fighting skill score to the total of the dice. If the grand total is 11 or more, turn to **126**. If the total is less than 11, subtract 4 hit points from your hit point total and turn to **21**. Remember that you may try to hit the draconian more than once, as long as you subtract 4 points each time you miss. Also remember than you may spend experience points to increase your chances at any time as long as you decide before the dice roll and subtract them from your total experience points after you use them.

121

"Before we leave the citadel, I think we should try to learn as much as we can about Verminaard's plans," you tell the others. Willow grins in delight, and Kegan gives you the most serious look you've ever seen on the young boy's face.

"And let's repay him for what happened to Solace!" Kegan says with a grim nod.

"Good!" Willow says, her kender eyes dancing with excitement. "Follow me. I know the way."

She opens the door to the hall carefully and checks for dragonmen guards. Then she darts into the carpeted corridor and walks quickly past a stone stairwell descending to a dimly lit landing.

"What's down there?" you ask her.

"Just the cellar. There're only a few storerooms and the women's prison. But there's no way out."

You motion for Kegan to follow and trot noiselessly behind the kender. The hallway turns sharply to the left, then broadens into a spacious corridor nearly forty feet wide that runs straight to the far end of the tower. The three of you have already rounded the corner before you spot two large hobgoblins standing outside some massive double doors halfway down the hall on the right. Turn to **94**.

122

The red design begins to fade, as if it were sinking into the surface of the stone. At the same instant, the thick panel begins to move, pivoting open from its center so that there are two narrow entrances, one on either side of the secret door.

"Quick!" Essa whispers. "The spell may not last very long!"

The slender maiden slips through one side of the stone panel while Kegan and Willow go through the other. With a little more difficulty, you squeeze your larger body past the wall. Just as you join your companions on the opposite side, the heavy door swings back into place with a low grinding sound.

"Whew!" you gasp. "A heavy man couldn't make it through there at all! Whoever built this place never

118

designed it for comfort!"

"My people have never been large," Essa says softly, "nor have their dwarven allies. But look ahead! Perhaps the next door will be more your size, Bern."

In the enchanted light, you see a large panel of tarnished bronze, embossed in gold with a beautifully sculpted relief of the head of a unicorn.

"It's the symbol of Kith-Kanan!" she whispers. The gentleness has returned to her face, and her wild green eyes are moist with emotion. "This is the entrance to the holiest place in elfendom—the tomb of Kith-Kanan!"

"Is it open?" Willow asks excitedly, her husky voice contrasting with Essa's soft tones. "Try it, Essa!"

The elven mage presses lightly on the dull metal. Despite centuries of devastation during and after the Cataclysm, the perfectly made door swings open noiselessly, as if it were oiled daily. Turn to **142**.

123

You twist away, parrying its thrust, and leap across the pool of acid. The dragonman's wings flare, and for a moment it seems to float above the pool. Then you hear a whistling sound and a soft thud. A small hole appears in the draconian's scaly face, just above its fan-shaped ears. Its wings fold suddenly, and the monster collapses into the acid gore of its companions. At the sight, the four dragonmen at the door flee in terror. You glance to the side and see Willow smiling as she returns her hoopak sling to her belt.

"Lucky shot!" you say with a grin.

"Lucky for you!" the kender retorts.

"Let's get out of here before we run out of luck!" Kegan interjects. You both smile and start for the door.

119

"Wait," says Willow. "Did you get the potions?"

You glance around, only to see the last of the vials dissolving in the acid pool. "They're gone!" you exclaim.

"Never mind," the kender replies. Turn to **100**.

124

You raise your head to look, but the pain is almost unbearable. Willow sees you collapse and cradles your head lightly in her hands. The coolness of metal touches your forehead as a golden medallion hanging from the kender's neck brushes your skin.

"Lie still, Bern," she orders. "That head wound looks terrible."

Suddenly you feel the gold medallion begin to pulsate with a strange warmth. It seems to flow into your forehead and on into your very brain. You feel as if every nerve cell in your head is aglow, and you see that a very soft light has started to throb inside the medallion. You feel the pain inside your head begin to diminish as the warmth increases. Soon the glow is strong enough to reflect the shocked, wide-eyed look of surprise on the young kender's freckled face beneath her coppery red hair.

You may make a single healing throw. Roll one die and add the number to your total hit points, then turn to **71**.

"The running prints overlie the ones going back the other way," you tell your companions. "Whoever made them was fleeing from something and seemed to know just which way to run. The left-hand passage must be the way out of the Sla-Mori!"

"That's what I tried to tell you!" chides Willow. "Bring your light over here, Essa, so we can see well enough to find the back door out of this place!"

The lovely sorceress frowns at the kender and glances to the right. You can see that for some reason she's reluctant to take the left branch of the corridor. Having witnessed her strange powers, you wonder if her hesitation may be due to some kind of magical awareness.

"What is it, Essa? Do you sense danger this way?"

The elven mage shakes her head, but the troubled look remains in her wild eyes. "It's nothing. You're probably correct about the tracks in the dust. Come on."

Without another word, the slender woman squeezes past Willow to join you and Kegan. Her silver aura fills the narrow rock passage, leaving the intersection behind you in darkness.

The tracks continue down the twisting corridor, leading you directly toward a bare rock wall. You glance around quickly, but you see no other tunnel or exit.

"Look, Bern!" Kegan says excitedly. "The tracks lead right up to that wall. There must be a secret door here!"

What your brother says must be true. The bootprints you've been following seem to pass straight through the wall of the cramped tunnel. You press yourself against its rough surface, listening for sounds on the other side.

"I can't hear anything," you report. "But Kegan's right. There's got to be a way to move this wall!"

The four of you make repeated attempts to locate a hidden opening in the dead-end passage but find nothing.

"It's no use looking here any more," you say finally. "Let's go back to the intersection and study those prints some more." When you've retraced your steps to the corridor leading from the zombie chamber, you kneel in the dust to examine the tracks once more. Turn to **84**.

126

Before the startled dragonman facing you can react, you stab it through the chest with your sword, Fireborn. The creature screams horribly, clutching at its chest. Green blood oozes through its fingers, and it slumps to the ground. You grab your sword to strike the other hideous creature.

But to your horror, you discover that your sword is stuck fast! The body of the first dragonman has turned to stone! Tugging at your sword in panic, you suddenly feel a burning pain in your back. You turn to see the other dragonman, its sword in hand, the weapon's blade stained red with blood—your blood. Slowly you sink into the dust in the road. You are thankful when darkness closes over you at last.

127

You have fought wild dogs and wolves in the forests near Crystalmir, and you are ready for the charge of the two war dogs. Ducking beneath the first, you grab its leather armor and fling the beast over your head. At the same time, you lunge upward with Fireborn just as the second war dog leaps for your arm. The first beast slams into the ground as its compan-

ion is impaled on your blade. You fling the dead animal from your sword and step quickly to the side of the stunned first dog before it can recover its breath. Fireborn slices through the spiked collar as if it were cloth, severing the beast's jugular vein before it can let out a whimper. Turn to **75**.

128

For the first time since you returned, you're glad that your battle armor is still back in Solace. In your Ranger's hunting leathers, you soon outdistance your pursuers. Their spears land at your feet, but you dodge them nimbly. In a few more steps, you've reached the rugged slope, and you begin to climb out of their range to safety.

At the top of the cliff, you bear to the right, away from the quarries. Soon you're trotting effortlessly along a forested ridge. When you're sure that the guards aren't following, you relax against a giant mountain pine and begin to plan your next move.

The evil forces at Pax Tharkas are much more powerful than you had imagined, and you decide that you must try to recruit enough warriors to invade the fortress. You wonder how much of Ansalon remains free of this powerful Dragon Highlord's influence.

You think immediately of the Qualinesti elves. You know they are a secretive and suspicious folk, but you may be able to convince them of the danger of the evil forces that threaten their forest homeland. Whether or not the elves are willing to help, you must do whatever you can to end Verminaard's menace and to rescue Kegan and the others from the slave pits of Pax Tharkas.

Congratulations for escaping from Pax Tharkas alive. Reward yourself with one extra experience point the next time you play the adventure.

129

The carrion crawler's eight writhing tentacles whip past your vicious blows, deflecting Fireborn's razor edge off the creature's armored head. Two of the tentacles wrap around your sword arm, pulling you off balance and tugging you toward the hungry scavenger.

"Get back, Bern! Its poison will paralyze you!"

Willow's warning comes just as as the crawler's gummy secretions cover your nostrils and mouth. A cold numbness penetrates through every muscle in your body. Fireborn clatters to the stone floor only seconds before the monster's tentacles drag you through the doorway into the darkness of the zombie crypt.

130

You leave the road hesitantly, then scramble into a ditch, your hand on the hilt of your sword. You're startled to see an old woman peering cautiously at you. Her face is smudged with sweat and ashes, but you recognize Cleva's shriveled, wrinkled features. Cleva is a distant cousin, one of your dead mother's kinswomen.

"What is it, Cleva? What terrible thing has happened here?"

The aged woman collapses against your shoulder,

sobbing desperately. It is several minutes before she can control her shaking body enough to speak in a hoarse whisper.

"They came down from the sky—great red beasts with wings as large as houses! Everywhere they went, they cast darkness and breathed fire!"

"Wait, Cleva!" you whisper. "You're not making any sense! Perhaps it was only a night—"

"A nightmare? Yes, it was a nightmare—a nightmare come true! As real as the blood of my sister that pumps through both our hearts, Bern Vallenshield! I woke to the cries of children leaping to their deaths from the flaming boughs of their tree homes! I stood below and watched the monsters rain fire and death upon our people! They were dragons, I tell you! The dragons of our darkest legends have returned to Krynn!" Turn to **200**.

131

"We have to risk the cellar," you say quickly. "The guards know we're in the tower, and they'll be up here soon! Quick! Let's find a place to hide!"

The kender nods and heads for the staircase, her coppery hair bouncing around her excited face. You hear the agitated voices of hobgoblins and draconians from the hallway, and you push Kegan's shoulder toward the cellar. Willow is already waiting at the bottom of the steps when you and your brother reach the landing. She's standing before a narrow door barricaded with a heavy timber.

"This is a kitchen storeroom," says the Kender. "We might be able to hide in here!"

"No," you tell her. "They'd notice the bar was gone and look in there right away! Where else can we go?"

"I could take you to the women's cells. They'd never look for you there, and I could pretend that I've been there since this morning."

"But it could mean a lot of trouble for the women if they did find us there," you object. "What else is down here?"

"Only a guardroom and the gully dwarves' quarters," replies the kender.

If you think that you should hide in the women's prison, turn to **46**. But if you elect to ask the gully dwarves to help you, turn to **64**.

132

In the shadowy interiors of the niches closest to your party, you glimpse slowly moving figures. As the first of the creatures steps from its crypt, your mind reels with horror. You find yourself staring at an undead thing, its cadaverous face ravaged by ages of decay, its gray, elven flesh dried and rotted. The stench of graves fills the corridor as more of the terrible creatures shamble from their crypts into the passage behind you. Only the corridor ahead remains empty of the living corpses, as if your passing footsteps have awakened them from their death sleep.

"Zombies!" cries Willow. "These creatures must serve as undead guardians of this place! I told you we shouldn't have come in here, Bern Vallenshield!"

If you choose to fight the zombies, turn to **184**. If

you have 10 or more hit points, you have enough strength to try to escape. Turn to **16**. The zombies are mindless and will not allow you to surrender.

133

The ancient fortress of Pax Tharkas is a massive stone structure with twin towers at each end of a huge wall and steps in the center of the wall leading to a central platform. The citadel straddles a mountain pass, so that the only ways to reach the valley behind it are either through the wall or over the steep mountain ridges. The only entrance you can see is a massive wooden portal in the center of the wall between the two towers.

The slave caravan winds its way past the front of the citadel, past the tower on the right, and into the mountains. Armed goblins are everywhere, and you see many of the squat draconians walking among them. You also see some much smaller figures, who seem to be working as laborers for the goblins and draconians. When the wagon gets closer, you see that they're dwarves of some kind, dressed in filthy rags and covered with mud and grease. Their skin is ravaged by sores and scars of pox and other diseases.

"What kind of dwarves are those, Bern?"

Kegan has joined you and Willow at the bars to

get his first glimpse of Pax Tharkas. "They're Aghar—also known as gully dwarves," says Willow in a low voice. "They live like parasites in many parts of Krynn. I've seen them before. Disgusting creatures, and stupid as rocks, but I've always heard they remember everything they've ever seen and will sell information at the drop of a coin."

The caravan weaves its way up the steep slopes on a narrow track that opens onto a wide mountain meadow behind the fortress. Here the wagon train rumbles to a stop outside the rear of one tower. Immediately you see a squad of hobgoblins marching toward the caravan. Turn to **157**.

134

"Hey! Let go! Who are you, anyway?" You struggle to free yourself, but it's hopeless. Although you are strong and skilled in fighting, you are no match for these men, whoever they are. You can't even see their faces because of their hoods. They hold you firmly, one behind you, the other in front of you.

"Who we are is not important," the one in front of you says in a strange, hissing voice. "What *is* important is that it is illegal to walk on the road."

"Since when?" you shout angrily.

"Since *we* took over!" he replies, laughing evilly. The strangers remove their hoods, and you see with horror that they are not men at all but some sort of terrible cross between man and reptile! Their faces remind you of pictures you have seen in ancient books about the legendary dragons of Krynn. But dragons never existed! You wonder if you are going mad!

The dragonman in front of you releases its grip, only to raise the hilt of the sword it carries. Obviously it intends to strike you with it.

If you decide to simply take the blow, knowing you can't fight two of these strange creatures, turn to **101**. But if you elect to fight these horrible creatures, turn to **120**.

135

"Gee," you say, looking worriedly down at the hobgoblin. "I hope the guards don't think the stew made him sick."

The gully dwarves stop their looting and look up at you. "Our stew not make sick!" the cook says indignantly. "Our stew good stew. All natural stuff!"

"I just hope Lord Verminaard realizes that," you say, heaving a great sigh.

The gully dwarves exchange nervous glances. "Uh, you get hobgoblin out of here," the cook says finally. Turn to **30**.

136

With a sudden surge of dark energy, the spectral form tries to rush the kender girl. You strike it fiercely with the sorceress's magical weapon just as it reaches out toward Willow's face. Suddenly the wraith's body seems to dissolve before your very eyes! At the precise instant the creature vanishes, the cavern air immediately feels warmer and fresher.

"It's gone for good," Essa declares. "It couldn't face the power of Willow's talisman after Bern weakened it with the silver sword."

"We've wasted enough time," says the impatient kender. Let's go back to the intersection and take the other passage!" By the time Essa has reclaimed her sword of crystal and silver, Willow is already groping her way into the dark tunnel.

You follow the left-hand passage and find that it leads almost immediately to the tunnel at the far end of the zombie hall. Willow is waiting for you, her back pressed against the rock wall. She gestures to the right, where the tunnel leads away from the corridor containing the crypts of the monsters.

"That's the only way out, unless you want to wake up our undead friends again," she whispers with a grin. Turn to **59**.

137

"Tell me what this 'Pax Tharkas' place is and why they're taking us there, Willow," you ask.

"All I know about Pax Tharkas is what I've heard in folktales and legends," replies Willow. "It's an ancient fortress high in the southern mountains, built by Kith-Kanan's elves of Qualinesti and Thorbardin's dwarves as a monument to the truce between their peoples."

"Maybe the dragons came from Qualinesti," you say. "I never did trust elves!"

"You know better than that, Ranger!" Willow says vehemently. "That crack on your head must have knocked something loose in your brain! There's far more evil in this than you could find in all of the Qualinesti forest! I can't imagine an elf having anything to do with hobgoblins and dragons, and neither can you, Bern Vallenshield!"

"Perhaps some of these mysteries will be solved when we reach Pax Tharkas," you mumble. You had forgotten the kender knack for insults and sarcasm.

"Then we'll have some answers soon enough!" Willow goes on. "I can see the towers of Pax Tharkas just ahead!" Turn to **124**.

138

The fortress is quiet, with only a few night guards patrolling the top of the battlements above. You realize angrily that Lord Verminaard must feel very secure. Well, maybe if you can escape, you can change all that! Hurriedly you drop the hobgoblin to the ground and unbuckle your sword belt from around its flabby stomach. As you do so, the hobgoblin mumbles and begins to stir, and you realize it is starting to come out of its stupor! You've got to act fast!

You know you haven't much time. Strapping Fireborn to your waist, you start to make a run for the hills to the south. Behind you, you hear the befuddled hobgoblin stagger to its feet.

Roll one die to see if you escape successfully. Add your physical prowess score to the die roll. If the result is 7 or more, turn to **72**. If it is less than 7, turn to **170**.

139

The armored head of the huge scavenger lunges toward you, its eight tentacles waving in your face and dripping the creature's paralyzing secretions. Fireborn flashes in Essa's magical aura, severing one of the writhing tentacles.

You dodge as a blob of the poisonous fluid flies across the corridor. With a vicious backswing, you strike the monster's carapace, scoring a direct hit above its left eye. To your amazement, the legendary blade only stuns the beast. The crawler's tentacles droop slightly as its head wobbles momentarily in the door frame.

"Close the crypt!" you yell, realizing that the carrion crawler's position makes it impossible for you to strike a vulnerable spot.

Before the creature can recover from your blow, Willow and Kegan rush forward to the stone slab and slam it against the crawler's tentacled head. You add your strength to their efforts, and together you manage to swing the heavy door completely shut against the monster's massive body.

"Move off to the side!" Essa commands.

The quiet urgency in the elven mage's voice compels all of you to do as she says. Essa steps closer to

the slab, placing her delicate hand on its rough surface. Then she whispers the same phrase you heard her use earlier on the door to the dragonmen's guardroom. Just as before, a thin golden line shoots around the sill of the tomb, flaring for an instant, then disappears.

"The crypt is sealed once more," she says quickly, "but I don't know how long it will be able to stop such a creature."

"Never mind that one!" shouts Willow. "Look!"

All around you, the other slabs have begun to slide open again, as if Essa's new spell has awakened the zombies once more. Turn to **16**.

140

From your hiding place on the bank of a river, you spot Kegan's wiry figure, a full head taller than the other children his age. Your brother is helping some of the women gather firewood.

Then you see one of the goblins hand Kegan a bucket and shove him toward the river. That gives you an idea of how to distract the hobgoblins and free the hostages, but it will put your younger brother in some danger. Then again, you might be able to do it without him.

If you decide not to risk your brother's life and go on alone, turn to **169**. On the other hand, your brother's already in danger, and this could be your only chance to free him and the others. If you decide it's worth the risk to his life, turn to **167**.

141

"It's too late to hide!" you whisper to the kender. "They've already seen us. We'll have to bluff our way past them!"

The two large hobgoblins are watching the three of

you closely from the niche by the doors to Verminaard's throne room. You motion for Willow and Kegan to follow you and start walking down the long hallway. When you approach their post, you call to them confidently, "I have a message for the Dragon Highlord from Fewmaster Toede!"

"Lord Verminaard is in the throne room and can't be disturbed, human!" growls one guard. Both hobgoblins are holding their pikes crossed in front of them, barring the doors of the council chamber.

"Where have you come from, and what's that child doing here?" demands the other monster.

You can tell the guards are getting suspicious. If you continue to try to bluff your way by them, turn to **36**. But if you decide this is getting you nowhere and choose to attack the guards, turn to **62**.

142

Once inside, no one speaks. You're all overwhelmed by the grandeur of what you see. You're in a huge hall, over a hundred feet wide. Rows of hand-carved granite columns extend upward into the darkness but leave the entire center of the chamber completely empty. Your party stays together, gathered around Essa's magic light, as you explore the cavernous chamber that, by some miracle of workmanship or magic or both, has remained intact since before the Cataclysm!

In the distance, the chamber narrows to a corridor between twin rows of columns. At the far end of the corridor, you see two massive bronze doors. Along the wall nearest you, behind the columns, you see another door, identical to the one you've just entered from the secret passage.

"We might as well check this door while we're on this side of the room," says Willow. "Bring that light of yours over here, Essa!"

The fearless kender has already reached the door on your side of the great chamber. By the time you and the others join her, she has opened it. The door opens into a short corridor that stops in front of another bronze panel only fifty or sixty feet away. Both doors are emblazoned with the crest of Kith-Kanan.

"I think we've come into the tomb by the back way!" Willow exclaims in a hushed whisper. "I've seen tombs built like this before, with several doors in the same passage. I think we've found Kith-Kanan's last resting place, Essa!"

The curious kender starts to push forward into the short passage, but the sorceress stops her with a hasty warning.

"If that is the tomb of Kith-Kanan, that passage may be trapped to thwart grave robbers!"

"I've been inside sealed tombs before," the kender replies, shaking her auburn pigtails. "If there are any traps in the Sla-Mori, I'll wager they're on the other side of those doors and we've avoided them by coming in the back way. What do you think, Bern?"

If you think you should heed Essa's warning and avoid the short corridor, turn to **98**. But if you think it is safe to proceed into the passage to the second bronze door, turn to **39**.

143

The vial with the dark red fluid seems somehow evil, perhaps because it is the color of blood. Desperately you uncork one of the milky potions and toss it down your throat. The thin liquid tastes watery and sour. You wait for a moment, watching the dragonmen crowd into the room, but you feel nothing. Then you bite the stopper from the other bottle containing the milky potion and swallow it, too.

You have just taken a double dose of a special healing potion. Roll one die four times (or two dice twice) for healing, add the grand total to your hit points, then turn to **60**. Remember that your total hit points may not exceed the number you started with.

144

"What you say makes sense, Cleva," you say reluctantly. "I can't help Kegan if I get captured. But what can I do? I feel so helpless! Isn't there some way to fight these monsters?"

"Some of the Seeker guards managed to escape when the dragons attacked," Cleva replies slowly. "I've heard they've joined with a group of resistance fighters near the elven lands of Qualinesti. They're led by—let me see, what was his name?" She mutters to herself for a moment. "Eben! That's it! Eben Shatterstone!"

"Thanks for all your help, Cleva," you say. "What will you do now?"

"Don't worry about me, Bern," Cleva says. "I'll be all right. You'd best be on your way."

You take one last look at your burned-out home. Then, your eyes misty with bitter tears, you plunge into the forest and begin the long trek south to find Eben Shatterstone.

145

The draconians swarm into Verminaard's bed-chamber, their broadswords upraised. You count seven of them—too many to fight, especially in the cramped chamber. You toss the scroll on the desk and reach for the chest of glass vials. Potions are rare in Solace, but you've heard of the wondrous effects, some deadly, that ancient mages produced with their powerful distillations. You decide that your predicament is desperate enough to risk an unknown potion, but you hesitate an instant before selecting one of them.

If you choose to drink one of the milky potions, turn to **143**. But if you drink the dark red potion, turn to **183**.

146

Finding a secluded thicket in which to hide the dapple mare, you lie on the sandy ground near the river and fall into an exhausted sleep. The sound of shouts and hooves wakes you at sunrise. You part the underbrush and see draconians walking through the goblin camp, kicking them and ordering them to their feet. You hear Toede's ugly little henchmen cursing and trying to make the dragonmen leave them alone, but their pleas are unsuccessful. You notice that none of the goblins even raises a hand to strike a draconian, no matter how angry the hotheaded creatures become.

Soon the caravan is rolling southward again, past your hiding place in the thicket. You mount the dapple mare again and begin to follow the slow-moving wagons. By the time the sun begins to disappear below the thick canopy of trees to the west, you can see snow-capped peaks in the distant south. The caravan begins to move more slowly, threading its way among shadowy ravines and canyons. You know that it will soon be too dark to travel in these hills because of the steep drop-offs on both sides of the road. The goblins will be forced to camp again. It looks like a perfect place for your rescue attempt.

Turn to **11**.

147

"Stop! It's—it's no use!" you cry. "I can't possibly win. I surrender!" You drop Fireborn to the floor.

"A wise decision," the Dragon Highlord hisses, and you imagine you see the face on his visor curl into a sneer. "Guards! Take this fool away!"

You turn just in time to see one of the draconian guards behind you, the shaft of its upraised pike descending straight toward your head, then everything goes black. Roll one die for damage, subtract the result from your total hit points, and turn to **17**.

148

When you return to consciousness, your first sensation is of incredible coldness. Then you realize that you're buried in a snowdrift. Later, after digging yourself out of the drift, you remember thinking that night was lasting an awfully long time, because it was pitch dark when you emerged from the snow-drift, and it still is.

But that was three days ago, and you still haven't seen the sunlight! There is a huge gash on the back of your head, and you've finally been forced to conclude that you're blind! Soon you know that hunger will drive you deeper into these unfamiliar forests, where you may find grass, bark, and insects to keep you alive until someone finds you. But right now, with the howls of timber wolves in the wilderness surrounding you, you'd welcome even a goblin patrol.

149

You are nearly halfway across the room, moving as silently as the kender, when suddenly you stumble and fall to your knees, your sword clanging loudly against the floor.

The door to the children's room flies open, and a flood of light cascades across the dragon's snout. The children see you and begin to yell, "Hey, Kegan, it's your brother!"

Kegan comes racing to the door, peering at you from around the dragon's bulk as you stagger to your feet. Turn to **105**.

150

The evil wraith attacks you immediately, trying to drain your strength away before you can wound it seriously with Essa's enchanted blade. Blasts of freezing air numb your arms and legs, and your muscles become leaden weights that you can hardly move.

"I can't fight it!" you scream through shivering lips. "Run for the tunnel!" The elven sorceress waits until Willow and Kegan have reached the cavern opening, then turns and utters a single spell word. Instantly fiery missiles spring from her fingertips, and you seize the chance to flee from the wraith. The magic missiles seem to confuse the spectral creature, and it darts back into the far shadows of the cavern.

The four of you race for the intersection and hurry down the left-hand branch. It ends only fifty feet down the corridor, at the rocky exit from the zombie chamber.

"Careful!" you whisper to Willow, who is already peering curiously into the hall of crypts. "We don't want to tangle with those creatures again! Head the other way before the wraith decides to follow us!" Turn to **59**.

151

Your first desperate slash with Fireborn strikes the griffon's side where its feathers merge with the fur of its hind section. The monster's whole body convulses with pain and you feel its talons suddenly open. You feel yourself begin to drop, and you grab desperately for the creature's breastfeathers, but it's too late! You see the forested hillside rushing up to meet your tumbling body, and you try to prepare yourself for the worst.

Just when you think the crushing blow must come

any second, your body is suddenly jerked upward, snapping your arms and legs in the air like the end of a bullwhip. It's the griffon, returning to recapture the meal it thought it had lost! The monster's wound is only a scratch, but it's painful enough to slow it down. You realize suddenly that you must strike while you're close enough to the ground to fall without getting killed. In desperation, you hack at the giant's taloned foreleg. Once more Fireborn finds its mark, and the griffon drops you again!

This time you land in a snowdrift and begin to career down the steep mountain slope like a runaway sled. You never see the rock until you feel its terrible weight slam into your back. Then blackness descends. Turn to **148**.

152

You need a weapon of some kind to intimidate these creatures, so you grab the nearest thing you can—a potful of stew. "Stand aside!" you shout menacingly, brandishing the pot. "That sword is mine!"

The gully dwarves stop looting the hobgoblin's unconscious body and look up at you, their mouths gaping open. Then their eyes brighten.

"Stew fight!" yells one excitedly, and before you know what is happening, the gully dwarves are grabbing spoons and bowls. Soon great globs of the foul mixture fill the air. In vain you try to stop them. Their whoops and hollers fill the air, and you know the guards will be here momentarily. A glob hits you in the face, and you can feel stew dripping from your ears. It covers the walls and floors. You try to reach the hobgoblin to grab your sword, but another glob of stew hits you in the eyes, blinding you. Then you hear the guards enter. The gully dwarves all begin to yell at once.

"He start it!" "It his fault!"

Wiping goo from your eyes, you see them all pointing at you. The hobgoblin guards, snarling, step into the room and spot their captain on the floor.

"So, trying to escape, eh?" one snarls. "We've had just about enough of you, Ranger! Since you're already covered with gravy, I think it's about time you feed the dragon!"

You don't quite know what this means, but it doesn't sound good. As the guards march you out of the kitchen, you hear one of the gully dwarves sigh.

"Too bad," he says wistfully. "He was fun guy."

153

You gallop southward for hours, until the terrain becomes too rough to travel fast. Then you guide the mare deeper into the mountains, not daring to pause to get your bearings, until you notice your mount starting to give out from the fatigue of keeping her footing on the rocky ground. Finally you stop the tired animal and dismount, leading her slowly forward until you hear the sound of trickling water.

Just ahead, you find a small mountain spring rushing from the snow-capped peaks above. It seems to be a safe place to rest, and the spring water tastes sweeter than any wine you have ever drunk. You sit with your back against a boulder, Fireborn laid across your lap, watching the thirsty horse get her fill of the icy water. Before you realize it, you have fallen asleep. Roll one die for healing, add the number to your hit points, and turn to **42**.

154

You all look quickly at the kender, who has been searching the crypt while you were listening at the doorway. She's crouched down between two empty stone biers, peering into a dark tunnel only a few feet high.

"It looks like a tight squeeze, but we can do it," she says. "Let me go first, with Essa behind to light the way." Without waiting for a reply, Willow crawls into the hole. Essa glances at you, shrugs, and drops to her knees to follow the kender. You push Kegan forward, then wedge yourself into the cramped passage behind them all.

After you've crawled for perhaps a dozen yards, the tunnel opens into a ten-foot-wide passage with a ceiling high enough to stand upright. The new corridor turns sharply to the left and continues straight ahead for about fifty yards.

"Uh-oh," mutters Willow from her place at the front of your group. "Which way do we go now?"

You squeeze past the others to join the kender at a junction of two passages carved out of the granite beneath Pax Tharkas.

"Sharpen those eyes, Ranger, and guide us out of here," urges Willow. The kender's husky voice lacks even a trace of concern. Ignoring her, you study each of the passages for some clue to the best route. You see tracks of small rodents everywhere in the corridor leading to the left, but nothing at all has disturbed the dust of the one on the right.

If you decide to take the left-hand passage, where you see the rodent tracks, turn to **182**. If you elect to try the right-hand passage, where there are no tracks at all, turn to **112**.

155

"Run!" you yell, knocking the hobgoblin to the floor with the flat of your sword. "Dragonmen!"

Before the draconian can draw its sword or summon more of the winged monsters, the three of you race for the stairs leading to the cellar. At the corner of the corridor, Willow stops and fires two more of her deadly missiles into the midst of the draconians storming out of the guardroom across from Verminaard's council chamber. They dive for the floor, giving you all time to reach the staircase.

Turn to **131**.

156

The two snarling war dogs leap for your throat simultaneously. Fireborn flashes in a wide arc, striking the first animal in the side, tearing the studded leather armor as if it were tissue. You dodge the falling corpse, which knocks the other war dog to the ground. Before you can silence the second beast, it begins to growl and bark viciously.

You know that the war dog's alarm will bring its draconian masters before you can kill it. Your only hope of releasing the prisoners depends upon your remaining free. With a glance at the captured warriors, you turn and dart into the shadows behind the wagon—only to see a dark figure with wings leap into your path. Turn to **96**.

"You! The big one who likes to fight! Out!" The hob-goblin captain waits until you've jumped from the wagon, then pushes you forward, toward the prison cart with the other men of Solace. As you climb into the prison wagon, you see that Willow and Kegan are being marched into the citadel by the goblins, along with the other women and children.

Inside the men's wagon, the men of your village greet you. They tell you how glad they are that you tried to help, even if it proved unsuccessful.

"Somehow we'll find a way to escape from this place and from whoever—or whatever—rules it," you vow in a whisper. "We couldn't save Solace, but we can avenge its destruction! Let each of you remember well those blackened vallenwood stumps and the cries of our children, then swear vengeance upon whatever evil forces were behind such treachery."

"We can't fight these monsters until our women and children are safe!" says one of the men. "Those creatures aren't human. They'd kill our families in the blink of an eye if we tried anything!"

The wagon rolls past a gaping cavern in the side of the mountain on one side of the narrow plain behind the citadel. A stench of sulphur spreads throughout the narrow valley. It seems to be coming from the huge opening. The mouth of the cavern is bustling with the activities of the gully dwarves, who appear to be moving great mounds of rock from a high ledge down to the level of the cave entrance.

On the ledge above, you see humans, naked to the waist, pulling cart after cart full of rocks to the wait-ing platform. Then the gully dwarves lower the rocks to their companions below.

The wagon continues past the laborers and stops at a second, even larger, cavern. Here a burly hobgoblin with two filthy gully dwarves at his side greets the driver of the prison cart.

"More of 'em, eh? We'll get every bit of that ore, if we have to sweat it out of all the humans left alive in Ansalon!"

The members of the hobgoblin squad laugh and approach the barred door of the wagon to let you and your companions out. The burly hobgoblin waits while the two Aghar servants search everyone completely, removing rings, armlets, armor, a few small knives, and even a small hatchet one of the warriors had hidden under his arm. When they dump the confiscated property in front of their master, he shakes his fist at all of you.

"You're here for one reason and one reason only—to serve Verminaard, Dragon Highlord of Ansalon! Before you are the legendary iron quarries of Pax Tharkas. The steel from these mines will be smithed into weapons of war to be used by those who follow our master. You will serve the Dragon Highlord's purposes by mining the ore, which will be smelted by the gully dwarves in the furnaces behind you. If anyone objects to this noble task, we will see to it that his family is treated with special care!"

The hobgoblin's sneer makes your skin prickle with silent rage. You must find a way to learn more about this mysterious person called Verminaard. His title of "Dragon Highlord" seems to suggest his involvement in the destruction of Solace. As the goblin teamster drives the prison wagon away, you study your new captors and think about escape.

The two gully dwarves are unarmed, and you know you could rout them both with little more than a battle cry. But the burly hobgoblin has the look of an old but seasoned warrior. Its hairy hide is more gray than black, and its faded eyes squint with age.

Though its scale armor is tarnished and rusted, the broadsword at its side is polished and well oiled. You know that you could not fight it without a weapon, but you might be able to outrun the aging monster.

If you have 29 or more hit points, you have strength enough to try to escape into the rugged country behind the mines. Turn to **34**. If you have less than 29 hit points, you must stay and regain your strength while you try to learn more about Pax Tharkas. Turn to **78**.

158
"Into the crypt! Quick!" you shout, clambering over the slain crawler as the zombies begin to emerge from their tombs all up and down the corridor. Essa is right behind you, her silver aura filling the small burial chamber with its ghostly light. Willow helps your brother step over the hideous carcass and follows him into the tomb.

As soon as everyone is inside, you grab two of the creature's stiffening legs and start to pull the carrion crawler away from the entrance to the crypt. With a disgusted frown, Kegan reaches for another of the scavenger's filthy pods and helps you. Essa and Willow pull the slab back in place only moments before the zombies outside reach the opening.

You stand beside the closed entrance with Fireborn raised high, prepared to strike the first undead creature to enter the crypt. For a tense moment, you expect to see the slab jerked aside by the monsters, but nothing happens.

"I think they're gone!" says Kegan, breaking the silence in the tomb.

"I doubt if they'll enter a closed crypt," Essa murmurs. "They've been stationed here to guard the outer hall. They have no minds of their own. They won't follow us."

"I'm more concerned about carrion crawlers!" you tell the elf. "If this one has been tunneling in these crypts long enough, it may have laid its eggs in some of the zombies' corpses. We need to find a way out of here fast, before a swarm of these things finds us."

"This may be it," says Willow. "I think I've discovered how the crawler got into the tomb!" Turn to **154**.

159

The glowing tip of Verminaard's mace strikes your shoulder just as the Dragon Highlord whispers a curious word.

"Midnight!"

Although the blow is merely a glancing one, it has so much force that you're knocked to the floor. It feels as if the cleric has struck you with something heavier than lead.

Suddenly the council room dims. The light from the chandelier fades, plunging the chamber into total darkness. Your sword arm is useless from Verminaard's blow and dangles painfully from your crushed shoulder. You grope on the carpet for the steel blade, knowing you couldn't swing it even you could find it in the inky blackness.

"I have your weapon, Solacian!"

Verminaard's sinister voice sends a chill down your spine. Apparently he can see in the dark like elves and dwarves! You struggle to your feet, swinging out with your good arm in the direction of the voice.

"Come, come, Ranger! Don't force me to use Nightbringer again! My cursed mace has already made you blind. Would you like to be dead as well?"

You feel your eyes with your left hand. To your horror, you discover that they're wide open! You grope your way to the long table, where a lighted candelabra stood only moments before. You can feel the heat of the candles against your face, although you can't detect even a faint glow! Verminaard was telling the truth. You're a blind man with a crushed sword arm, and you have no hope left!

160

You are too frightened to attack this creature of legend. Instead, you turn and flee into the wilderness, trying to shut out from your ears the shrill screams of the horse you left behind.

Finally, exhausted, you can go no farther. You sink to the ground in despair. Your homeland has been destroyed by unknown evil creatures. Your brother is held prisoner as a slave in the mines of Pax Tharkas. And now you are out here alone and lost.

"Help me!" you plead, though you know your prayer is hopeless. The gods turned away from men long ago—at least, so Hederick, the High Theocrat of Solace, says.

But you begin to feel a great sense of peace surrounding you. "Help me!" you cry once more. "Please help me defeat this great evil!"

Suddenly a white stag appears before you. You sit up, staring in astonishment. It's the most magnificent animal you have ever seen. As you watch, the stag shakes its glistening horns and bounds off. Then it stops and looks back at you.

Stunned, you realize that the stag is waiting for you. Staggering to your feet, you start after the stag. You have no idea where it is leading you, but somehow you know that it will guide you safely on your journey. . . .

161

You see a windowless chamber, larger than the playroom, and you sense immediately that it isn't empty. In a shaft of light filtering into the room from an open door across the room, you see a massive hulk, rising and falling with regular wheezing noises. As your eyes become accustomed to the darkness, you suddenly realize what you're looking at. It's the enormous flank of a red dragon!

"That's Flamestrike," Willow whispers in your ear. "She's an ancient beast, scarred and nearly blind. She's also quite mad. Her own children were killed many years ago, and she's convinced that the slave children are *her* children. The Dragon Highlord told her that someone was trying to steal her broodlings again, in order to post her as a guard. The only other people she allows in here are Maritta and her women, who feed and tend to the children."

You dislike the risk of confronting this creature, however old and mad she may be, but you know that it is the only way to rescue your brother. Perhaps you can sneak past her while she sleeps. You step forward and start inching your way across the dragon's dark chamber toward the partially open door.

Roll one die to find out if you make it safely past the dragon. Add your observation skill score to the die roll. If the result is 6 or more, turn to **168**. If the result is less than 6, turn to **149**.

"Where did that creature come from?" Kegan asks the kender girl. "Was it just waiting there for us?"

"Crawlers are pretty stupid, Kegan," replies Willow. "My guess is that this one and more like it have honeycombed these crypts to feed on the undead carcasses of the zombies."

"If that's so, it couldn't have moved the slab because of whatever magic was used to seal the zombie guardians inside their tombs," Essa says quietly.

"Then that means there's got to be another way out of that crypt!" you murmur. "The crawler's tunnel may lead to the surface!"

"Or maybe into a whole nest of those things!" Kegan says with a shudder.

"Well, what are we waiting for?" Willow demands impatiently. "Let's find out how this bug got into the Sla-Mori!" Turn to **24**.

You know you've struck the Dragon Highlord several times with Fireborn, but each time, you are amazed to see the wound heal itself immediately! Suddenly the evil cleric steps back and points at you.

"Take him, Ember!" he commands the gigantic red dragon.

The terrible monster's nostrils begin to emit a thin stream of smoke as he rears his head and repositions his heavy bulk between you and Verminaard. You glance at Willow and Kegan, but they appear to be frozen, their glassy eyes staring straight ahead. Either the Dragon Highlord or his evil dragon has cast some kind of spell on your brother and the kender. Now only you stand between Verminaard and his plans to control all of Ansalon.

Before you can fight the dragon, you must first roll

two dice to attempt a saving throw against breath weapons. If you roll 7 or less, turn to **190**.

If you roll 8 or more, you must fight the dragon. Roll two dice to hit and add them to your fighting skill score. If the result is 12 or more, turn to **9**. If it is less than 12, deduct 10 hit points and turn to **190**. If you feel you are losing the fight, you may choose to surrender. Turn to **147**. If you have any experience points left, you may want to consider using them now.

164

The griffon's eyes glass over and start to blink. It has released your arm once more, and its flight is growing wobbly. You can feel the clutch of its talon around your waist weakening, and you have to grab at the mixture of fur and feathers at its breast to keep from falling to your death. Somehow the creature manages to stay aloft, with you clinging to it, for what seems an eternity. It soars on and on, past the snow-capped peaks to a place where the glaciers give way to forests on the other side of the mountains.

Finally the beast's wings falter and its great head droops to its chest. You hang on desperately to its breastfeathers as it plummets to the rocky slope below. Fortunately for you, the heavy carcass strikes the wooded hillside on its back, cushioning your body. You bounce high in the air and land once more on the griffon's soft underbelly, then slide to the ground, where you come to rest on a fragrant bed of pine needles, scarcely able to believe you're still alive.

When you're sure you can stand and look around, you see that none of the trees or shrubs are familiar. Even the rocks are different from any you've ever seen. The griffon has flown so far that you must have landed many hundreds of kilometers away from where you left the slave caravan. Even your Ranger's pathfinding skills can't help you find your way because you lost your bearings during the monster's flight.

Perhaps someday you'll be able to retrace the griffon's long flight and find the mysterious Pax Tharkas, where the goblins and dragonmen have taken your brother and the other survivors of the Solace catastrophe. But for now you will have enough of a problem just staying alive in this strange, cold land. . . .

165

"Do you think there are more draconians in there?" you whisper to Willow.

"There were several squads of them, plus a group of hobgoblins, when they brought us through here three nights ago," she replies. "I think this tower must be the main guardroom for the whole citadel, from what I've seen and heard."

"Then it would be foolish to attack them! Even if we surprised this bunch, the others would hear us and we'd be trapped! We'll have a better chance to

157

escape from the other tower."

The kender nods, her face revealing neither approval nor disappointment. She seems to be willing to support any decision you make, as long as it involves a challenge. "Let's go, then!" she says. Turn to **43**.

166

You slash frantically with Essa's magical sword, trying to slay the spectral wraith. The creature's shadowy form swirls around your struggling body, enveloping you in a dense cloud of freezing vapors.

"Get back, Bern!" Essa screams. "Don't let it touch you!"

You try to avoid the wraith's attack, but it's too late. Your strength is being sapped rapidly, leaving your arms as limp as rags. The monster's dark shape seems to surround you, blotting out the glare of the light from Essa's spell. Finally your frozen legs collapse beneath your weakened body just as the creature's blackness merges with your thoughtless mind.

167

You watch as Kegan walks slowly toward the stream with his bucket. The goblins appear to be relaxing after their dinner, quaffing from wineskins. They start to laugh among themselves at bawdy goblin jokes, winking whenever one of the younger girls from Solace passes by the campfire. You duck deeper into the shadows of the marsh grass and wait for your brother to dip the pail into the shallow water.

With the stealth of a snake, you creep closer. Quickly you clap your hand over Kegan's mouth from behind. The startled boy tries to scream and twist away, but you hold him tightly and stifle his cry.

"It's me, Bern!" you whisper urgently. "Don't make any noise!"

Kegan's face is a mixture of joy and anger when you release your grip on his mouth. "Don't attack *me!* Fight *them!*" he mutters. "Where have you been? I thought they must have killed you back in Solace!"

"Shhh! They'll wonder why you're not back with that water! You can complain all you want after we help the others escape. You'll have to do something to get those drunken oafs out of the way long enough to let me reach the shadows by the wagons."

"What do you want me to do?" Kegan asks excitedly, his anger vanishing with the promise of adventure. Turn to **31**.

168

You manage to reach the partially opened door without awakening the beast. As you push the portal gently, more light spills into the nursemaid's chamber and onto the beast's huge snout.

Just as Flamestrike's breathing begins to change, a shrill voice yells from inside the room. "It's Bern! Look, Kegan, it's your brother!"

"Shhh!" you whisper frantically.

"I'm afraid it's too late for that," says Willow in a hushed tone from alongside you. "Flamestrike's awake!"

Kegan squirms his shoulders between you and the kender, staring at the confused dragon. Turn to **105**.

169

You hide in the tall marsh grass by the river until your brother has filled his pail with water and returned to the goblin. Grinning, you watch as Kegan "accidentally" sloshes water over the goblin's feet. The creature swears loudly and knocks him flat

159

with a blow from its clawed hand.

You clench your fists in anger. There's nothing you can do but wait. The goblins settle down by the fire, passing around a wineskin. Before long they are obviously drunk, roaring with laughter and making crude comments whenever any of the women pass.

You realize that this is your chance. You sneak out of the marsh grass and make your way to one of the lead wagons, where some of the men from Solace are being held.

"Bern!" says one, recognizing you.

"Hush!" you whisper, taking out your knife and using it to pry at the lock.

"Bern, look out behind y—"

But the warning cry comes too late. You hear nothing more as pain explodes in your head. Roll one die for damage, subtract the total from your hit points, then turn to **114**.

170

"Stop, slave!"

Behind you, you hear the hobgoblin guard yelling for help. Desperately you run faster. You're nearly at the rugged slope when a dozen armed goblins emerge from the mouth of the smelter cave.

You stop in your tracks and glance back. The old

hobgoblin has almost caught up with you, moving much more quickly than you thought it could! There's nothing you can do but surrender to the monsters and face whatever punishment they give you for trying to escape.

The goblins swarm around you, their swords and spears bristling.

When their hobgoblin commander pushes through their ranks, it grabs a spear from one of its underlings and raises it above its head. You flinch reflexively, expecting to feel the steel tip bury itself deep inside your body.

Instead, the angry hobgoblin brings the heavy shaft down on your head with every ounce of its oafish strength.

Turn to **189**.

171

You're helpless in the grasp of the lionbird as it pulls your struggling body closer, clutching your chest with its other set of talons. Its huge wings fan the cold mountain air around you, and you feel the beast lift you as easily as a mother might lift her new baby. In the next instant, the griffon soars away into

the dawn sky. Far below, you spot the tiny dot of the fleeing horse you saved from this beast.

You twist in the monster's grasp, trying to get your arm free enough to use your sword. Finally the fabric of your sleeve tears away from the sharp talons. You can take this opportunity to try to escape from its clutches, or you can attack.

If you decide to attack, roll two dice to hit and add your fighting skill score to the result. If the total is 12 or more, turn to **48**. If your total is less than 12, subtract 5 hit points and turn to **65**. If your hit points are 20 or more, you have strength enough to try to escape at any point in the action. Turn to **151**.

172

You soon discover that the two hobgoblins are better trained than you had hoped. When you lunge toward the first, aiming below its pike for a belly strike, the second guard swings its long weapon and blocks your thrust. The action gives Willow time to use her hoopak. With a deft flip of her wrist, the girl sends one of the armor-piercing missiles flying at the second hobgoblin's head.

The stone strikes the monster just below its ear, shattering its jaw. The wounded creature howls with pain and tries to spit the kender on its pike. Just then, before you can retreat, a door across the hall bursts open and one of the draconians rushes into the corridor to investigate the hobgoblin's cry. Turn to **155**.

173

With a chill in your blood, you turn away from the pleading Cleva and, keeping to the woods, trot toward the western edge of town, where Solace's only blacksmith's shop is located. You're still several hundred yards away when you first hear the sounds of pitiful wailing. Cries of women and children mingle with harsh voices, speaking Common with a strange accent. Hiding among the burned stumps of the once mighty trees, you peer cautiously out at Theros Ironfeld's shop. The sight makes you gasp with horror. Turn to **69**.

174

Flamestrike points her nose at the ceiling and rolls her eyes in a trancelike state. A low rumbling sound stirs from her great belly, muffled at first but growing more distinct. Finally the rumbling takes the form of words, which you feel more than hear. A rosy glow surrounds the dragon's huge shape, revealing the scars of countless battles lining her ancient flanks.

> "Hear the curse of Mataflure,
>   Who calls the Queen to task.
>   Mother of Night, I thee abjure
>   To probe the face behind the mask.

> "Strike with fear, stark and pure,
>   Those who in lies do bask.
>   Suffer this eggling all harm to endure.
>   This, Queen Mother, does Mataflure ask."

Willow's face tightens as she leans toward you and whispers, "She's casting a spell to protect Kegan from anyone who speaks lies in his presence, and that includes us! Concentrate as hard as you can and try not to feel afraid. We kenders are immune to these things, but I've seen the bravest human warriors cringe in corners when confronted with such spells."

You must first attempt a saving throw against spells. Roll two dice. If you roll 6 or more, your throw is successful. Turn to **108**. But if you roll less than 6, you have failed your saving throw. Turn to **66**.

175

Moving quickly, you twist around just as the dragonman catches you. Before it has a chance to land on your back, you hack at its squat form. Fireborn's keen edge slices through the studded leather vest, and the creature drops the broadsword and collapses on the ground. You gasp as its body is transformed instantly into a stone statue! You stare at it in horror, thankful you didn't stab it with your sword or you would have lost your weapon as it became encased in stone!

Before the goblins can dodge the hardened corpse, you bound for your horse. The dapple mare snorts nervously as you leap into the saddle. Then she races away into the darkness. Turn to **153**.

176

No matter how hard you try, you cannot lift the iron bar across the doors. Frustrated, you stumble around the dark room until you find the door you came in. The hallway is still empty. You must return to the kitchen and try your other idea. Turn to **97**.

177

While Verminaard's attention is diverted by the draconians at the door, you charge the evil cleric with Fireborn flashing, keeping the Dragon Highlord between you and the great red dragon called Ember.

Verminaard dodges your blade easily and whips a heavy mace from his belt. You notice quickly that it's a curious weapon, carved of glistening black wood with silver streaks running through its grain. The spiked end seems to be made of some kind of crystal. It looks fragile, but it glows with an unnatural light in the Dragon Highlord's hand.

Roll two dice to hit and add the result to your fighting skill points. If the result is 13 or more, turn to **163**. If it is less than 13, deduct 5 hit points and turn to **159**.

If you are losing, you may surrender. Turn to **147**. There is no possibility of escape.

178

The confused hobgoblins respond to Willow's command as if she were their commander. When they leave, she breaks into a run for the end of the hall.

"Come on! Follow me to the cellar!" she calls in a whisper. You grab Kegan's hand and start after Willow. By the time you hear the shouts of the guards, you've reached the stairs.

"All they needed was a little direction," mutters the kender, "and all we needed was a head start. Let's get down these stairs!" Turn to **131**.

"The Dragon Highlord bids you greetings, good mother Mataflure!" you say in a loud voice, using Flamestrike's secret dragon name that she revealed to her "children." "He has commanded me to conduct one of your children to his chambers. Lord Verminaard wishes to honor you by training the nestling personally!"

"What do you mean, 'nestling'?" whispers Kegan, looking insulted.

"Just shut up and act like a dragon!" you say under your breath. Your brother looks at you as if you're crazy, while Willow chokes with laughter.

"I know nothing of this," rumbles Flamestrike. "Why was I not informed before now? Where is Maritta?"

"She's preparing breakfast, Mother," calls Willow. "She sent me to tell you about it, but you were asleep and I didn't want to disturb you."

The monster's cloudy eyes blink open a bit wider as it tries to recognize the kender. "I know that voice. You're one of my children."

"That's right, Mother. Just stay here and guard the other children. There are strangers about, and we must be very careful today. I'll take good care of your nestling and bring him back as soon as the Dragon Highlord permits it."

Flamestrike wavers, and you know that your trick has worked. You put your hand on Kegan's shoulder and begin to guide him around the monster's huge bulk. Turn to **110**.

You scream loudly and run to the mare's assistance, slicing at the griffon's taloned feet and furry haunch. The mare's reins finally snap with the force of her frenzied thrashing. The terrified horse leaps away from the monster just as your steel sword scores a glancing hit on the creature's hind leg. The wound infuriates the griffon, and it turns away from the fleeing mare and attacks you instead. You thrust your blade upward, hoping to plunge it into the creature's massive body, but its talons catch your arm! Turn to **171**.

181

Willow's youthful face is taut with excitement, and you can tell that she's bursting with curiosity about Verminaard's private chambers. You want to see the Dragon Highlord's rooms, too, if only to search for another way out of the citadel.

"We'll wait for his lordship in his rooms," you announce to the large hobgoblin. "Tell him why we're here as soon as possible!" Without waiting for a reply, you grab Kegan's arm and shove him roughly ahead of you toward the door at the end of the hall.

"Hey, watch it, B—"

"Quiet, child!" you interrupt, using the Solacian dialect. "They're already suspicious," you add under your breath. "Just act as if you hate me!"

"That'll be easy!" he replies vehemently in the same dialect. Willow's face is cracking into an uncontrollable smile that threatens to become a belly laugh at any moment. You hurry your brother into the Dragon Highlord's private suite and slam the door just as the girl's grin breaks into an squeal of delight. Turn to **68**.

"I don't trust a passage that even rats are afraid of," you murmur. "The corridor to the left looks like a better bet to me."

"Let's go, then!" says the impatient kender, stepping into the darkness without even waiting for Essa's magical aura to light the way.

"We'd better hurry before her curiosity kills her," you tell Essa and Kegan, urging them on.

The corridor continues in a straight line for only a short way. Then, just ahead, you see Willow pressing her small body against the granite wall at an intersection. The kender has her hand raised, motioning for you to keep quiet.

"We've run into the tunnel from the zombie chamber!" she whispers with a nod to the left. "Unless you want to wake them up again, I suggest we turn to the right. Let's have some more of that expert tracking, Ranger!"

You glare into her laughing eyes for a moment, then brush past her to examine the floor for signs of footprints. Turn to **59**.

If Willow was right about the white potions being healing potions, they'd be useless to you now. You might need a healing elixir later, but now you need something that will help you fight these draconians. Quickly you bite the cork from the vial with the dark red substance and suck the oily liquid and swallow.

The potion is salty and makes you gag violently, but you manage to keep it down. The guards are watching you strangely, trying to understand what you're doing. Finally they decide to close in and begin crowding you toward one of the corners of the bedchamber.

Just when you begin to doubt if the potion will have any effect at all, a pleasant warmth starts to spread from your stomach to your chest and limbs. The feeling grows steadily, filling your muscles with an instant surge of energy. Your brain is also affected by the potion, so that you're overwhelmed by a sensation of total power.

Shrieking a fierce battle cry, you charge headlong into the midst of the astonished dragonmen. You move among them like a berserker, swinging Fireborn again and again, so rapidly that the steel blade is nearly invisible. Forged by craftsmen from the heartmetal of a mountain, the steel blade dances in and out among the confused draconians, stabbing, gouging, hacking without mercy.

The draconians try to defend themselves, but your muscles seem to know precisely when to dodge their blows. The potion has made you an invincible fighter, at least for now, and before long the remaining draconians decide to try to escape from your one-man massacre.

You bound across the room with lightning speed, catching the two survivors in the doorway, and fell them both with one stroke of Fireborn's bloody blade. You whirl around, looking for more of the dragonmen to slay, but no more are left alive. Suddenly the corpses of the monsters begin to sizzle and smoke, then start to dissolve! In a matter of seconds, all that remains of each body is an oily pool of acid so powerful that even their swords and armor are disintegrating before your very eyes! Turn to **54**.

184

The zombies stalk toward the four of you, forcing you backward toward the end of the corridor. There are more of the undead creatures than you can count,

with still others emerging from the shadows at the other end of the passage. Their gaunt flesh is dressed in ancient armor, and they carry pale swords in their rotting hands.

"It's Kith-Kanan's Royal Guard!" Essa exclaims in a strangled voice. "We can't possibly fight them, Bern!" Turn to **55**.

185

"We can't go back now," you whisper to Willow and Kegan. "This may be our only chance to escape from Pax Tharkas. Those scaly things are half-drunk. We'll take them completely by surprise if we rush them!"

Willow nods and pulls her hoopak sling from beneath her cloak. "Stay behind me until they get close enough for your knife," she whispers to Kegan. The excited boy glances at Willow's fearless face and forces a tight-lipped smile to match hers.

"Be ready on the count of three!" you whisper. "One . . . two . . . *three!*"The number becomes a battle cry as you burst into the entry hall, hacking with Fireborn at the nearest two dragonmen.

Roll two dice to hit. Add your fighting skill score to the total. If the result is 12 or higher, turn to **85**. If it is less than 12, deduct 4 hit points and turn to **189**.

If at any time you feel you are in danger of being defeated, you may choose to surrender (turn to **51**) or try to escape (turn to **57**).

You bound into the shadows just as the other draconian bursts into view. The dragonman is scampering on all four limbs, using its wings to add speed to its pursuit. It carries a spiked ball in its mouth to free its hands for extra speed. The goblins are many yards behind, unable to keep up with it. You reach the shadows, but you realize the draconian might be able to catch you before you get to the horse.

If you have 22 or more hit points, you have strength enough to keep running. If this is your choice, turn to **3**. Or you may decide to turn and fight. Roll two dice to hit, then add your fighting skill score to the total. If the result is 12 or more, turn to **175**. If it is less than 12, deduct 4 hit points and turn to **53**.

"We can't risk returning to the mines to release the other warriors," you tell your companions. "That'll have to wait until we return to Pax Tharkas with reinforcements to fight the Dragon Highlord's forces. We're the only ones who know the connection between the dragons' attack and this place, and we've got to warn anyone who may still be able to resist Verminaard's forces."

"You're right, Bern," says Willow. "If we got captured trying to rescue the slaves, there'd be no one left to foil Verminaard's plans."

The evening shadows are lengthening steadily. Soon the small Krynnian sun will sink behind the quarries of Pax Tharkas, and you'll be able to pass through the scattered draconian and hobgoblin guards without being seen.

You're not sure if there'll be a town or village left untouched by Verminaard's horrible beasts in all of Ansalon, but somehow, somewhere, you'll find the help of enough warriors to end the Dragon Highlord's tyranny and rescue the slaves from the quarries of Pax Tharkas.

Congratulations on escaping alive. Reward yourself with one extra experience point next time you play the adventure.

188

Your blade cuts a deep gash into the shoulder of the first attacker, but three more goblins rush forward to help. They have you surrounded, backed up against the blackened tree stump, their steel weapons flashing in your face.

You know that goblins are poorly trained, unskilled fighters. Fireborn flashes in the sunlight as your first blow catches the nearest goblin's wrist, severing its sword hand from its arm. The edge of Fireborn is so sharp that the hand still clutches the sword's hilt as it falls to the ground. The goblin shrieks in agony, while its companions thrust it roughly aside. Dropping to one knee, you grab a handful of powdery dust and fling it into their faces.

They yell wildly and begin to stagger around, rubbing their eyes. You bound forward, screaming in rage. Your blade flashes in the morning sunlight, a deadly sliver of steel dancing among the dull-witted goblins. The goblins turn and race toward the road, screaming for help. You disappear back into the cover of the brush. Turn to **89**.

189

The shaft of the monster's weapon strikes your forehead a vicious blow. You struggle to remain conscious, but blackness overwhelms you. Roll one die for damage, deduct the result from your hit points, and turn to **17**.

190

The great beast of Krynn's legendary past follows every move of your body, his huge eyes unblinking all the while. The dragon's black tongue slithers forward, testing the air in front of you like some large poisonous snake.

"Taste this!" you scream, swinging Fireborn with all your strength at the monster's head.

Ember's giant head jerks to one side, and your blow barely nicks his snout. The blade's volcanic steel edge succeeds in gouging a slice of red dragon hide from the creature's nose, producing a flood of dark purple blood on the rich carpet.

In a frenzy of rage, Ember lets his mouth gape open, emitting a stream of suffocating gases that saturate the council chamber. Your lungs fill immediately with the burning fumes, making it impossible for you to breathe! You collapse in a coughing spasm, unable to do anything but gasp and retch violently. Your thoughts are fading rapidly, and you realize too late that it is useless to fight such a powerful creature with a normal weapon.

191

"They're bound to find you here," says a quiet voice from inside the cell.

The speaker's voice is so captivating that it silences the excited women immediately. You step closer into the shadows and see a delicate woman, lovelier than any you've ever known before. Her face is a perfect blend of feminine beauty, plus something wild that you can't name. Her unruly hair is an unusual silver shade you've seen only among the elves of the Qualinesti forest, and the tip of a pointed ear protrudes through the shimmering curls. The elven maiden is dressed in a simple tunic of lemon yellow deerskin that clings to her lithe figure like an exquisite gown.

"What do you mean, Essa?" demands Willow. The kender's exclamation tears your thoughts away from the elf's enchanting beauty.

"There's really no place to hide in here, and no way a disguise could transform the Ranger into a woman."

"Do you have a better suggestion?"

"Yes, I do. We can take you into the storage room and find a place to hide there. There's an ancient well inside that's large enough for several people to hide in."

You recall the small door inside the guardroom and nod excitedly. "Good! That way, we wouldn't be putting these women in any danger of punishment for hiding us. Thanks, Essa! If we ever manage to escape

176

from Pax Tharkas, I'll do everything I can to return for you—uh, all of you, that is!" you add, blushing as Willow snorts impatiently.

"No, Bern Vallenshield," Essa corrects. "*We* shall return. I'm going with you." The lovely woman's voice is so compelling that you say nothing, but Willow is not so enchanted by Essa's beauty.

"You'd only be in our way, Essa!" the kender says in a husky voice. "I'm sorry, but that's how it is. With you along, our moonstruck Ranger, here, would feel so obligated to protect his lady fair that he'd take foolish chances. Besides, you have no weapon, and we need strength, not another burden!"

"But I do have a weapon," replies Essa before you can say anything to Willow. You notice Essa's face change in the shadows in a way that is difficult for you to describe, except to say that it becomes wilder, more savage. A brilliant light appears in her outstretched hand for only an instant. When it vanishes, the elf is holding a gleaming dagger! The magical weapon is fashioned of the purest silver, and an unnatural glow surrounds it.

"You're a witch!" Willow exclaims.

"I prefer the word 'mage,' but let's not argue about labels," Essa replies quickly. "We really should be hiding, you know."

You warn the women to say nothing about what they have seen or heard. Then the four of you leave the cell amidst the stunned silence of the prisoners. Turn to **13**.

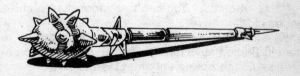

192

"Now that we're safe, we can find the entrance to the Sla-Mori," says Essa calmly. Her silver hair shines in the soft light of her spell, and her face has lost much of its gentleness.

" 'Sla-Mori'?" Willow repeats excitedly. "That sounds downright creepy!"

"Yes . . ." you add suspiciously as you spot the well. "A little too creepy. What is it, anyway?"

"The Sla-Mori is both the underground catacombs of the ancient elven people and the secret entrance into Pax Tharkas," she declares. "It's the burial chamber of the great Kith-Kanan, my people's first ruler and the founder of Qualinesti. It was Kith-Kanan who built Pax Tharkas with the help of the dwarves during the Age of Dreams. Later the Sla-Mori was sealed by the Cataclysm when the gods deserted Krynn, and it lies here, directly beneath the Dragon Highlord's citadel."

"How do you know all these things?" Willows asks excitedly.

"Yes," you add. "You can't be more than eighteen years old."

Essa smiles at you patiently. "You forget that I am an elf, Bern. I have lived in Krynn for almost eighty years, though I seem only eighteen to you."

You feel your face flush. It's difficult to think of this beautiful girl being so much older than you are! You realize, too, that she must be a high-level sorceress as well. Suddenly you feel very foolish, especially since you notice Willow looking at you with pity. Essa, seeing your embarrassment, continues her story as if you had not spoken.

"In Tarsis, I found an ancient scroll that spoke of the Sla-Mori. These legends have always been told among my people, but this parchment contained something new—it mentioned a well that Kith-Kanan ordered dug to quench his soldiers' thirst during the many sieges of Pax Tharkas. The scroll said that the well was just inside the fortress, by way of the Sla-Mori!"

"And you think this is that same well?" you ask, studying the wide hole in the floor intently.

"I'm certain of it. My people needed information about Pax Tharkas, so I volunteered to get 'captured' during Verminaarad's first raids so that I would be able to search the lower levels of the citadel. This is the only well I could find inside Pax Tharkas, and only a few of the gully dwarves know about it. The gully dwarves have been using it for a cesspool, dumping their filth into it to save them the trouble of hauling it up the stairs."

"So you decided to trick us into coming here so you could search for this Sla-Mori of yours!" you say with bitterness.

"I didn't want the others to know about such an important secret. Verminaard knows that the elves are seeking Wyrmslayer, and his forces would stop at nothing to prevent the elves from finding it."

"Wyrmslayer! What is *that?*" Kegan asks.

"The legendary sword of Kith-Kanan. Wyrmslayer is reputed to have special magical powers against dragons. My people say that it was buried with Kith-Kanan in the Sla-Mori."

The mage's tale would have sounded too fanciful for belief if you had not witnessed her magic. You glance at Willow to see what she thinks of Essa's story, but the kender is already moving crates and loose piles of junk away from the crumbled wall at the rear of the chamber. You have always heard that a kender's curiosity can never be satisfied, and you can see that Willow's interest has been more than aroused.

"Well, it's either find our way to the Sla-Mori, or wait until that spell wears off the door!" you exclaim, joining the search just as you hear the first shouts and blows of pounding fists through the thick panel.

Roll one die to find the secret door. Add your observation skill score to the result. If the total is 5 or over, turn to **40**. If it is less than 5, turn to **95**.

193

"Stop!" you cry. "I surrender! It was all my doing. I forced the others into helping me. I threatened to kill them if they didn't obey."

"That's not tr—" Kegan starts to say.

But Willow grabs your brother, and you hear her whisper swiftly, "Shut up, you little fool! Bern's not doing this to protect you! He's giving us a chance to try again! And next time"— she looks at you with grim determination—"we'll succeed!"

The draconians grab you roughly and chain your arms behind you. Then they look at Kegan and Willow. Kegan looks at you and gulps, then says, pretending to whimper, "That big bully scared me to death! I want to go back with the other kids, where I belong!"

"The kid's right," Willow says, blubbering with mock tears. "Bern made me come with him! I didn't want to."

The draconians stare at them dubiously, then shrug. "If it was me, I'd pick better companions than these two," one of them says to you, sneering.

"Yeah. I'll remember that next time, scale-face," you say, gritting your teeth and waiting for the blow you know is on the way. . . .

194

As you feel some of your strength begin to return, you give the talisman back to Willow and stand up. Kegan can only stare at you in awe, remembering your battle frenzy, but Willow merely shakes her head.

"If we had a gallon of that stuff, we could clean out Pax Tharkas by ourselves in no time!" she exclaims. "Of course, you might not live through the hangover!"

"I wonder what those other potions were," you say slowly.

"We'll never know. They fell into one of those puddles of draconian acid juice!" she replies. "But enough talk. Let's go before we have to fight more of those things without an extra shot of courage!" Turn to **100**.

195

The tunnel winds and twists for several hundred feet before it opens into a natural cavern with irregular walls. As soon as you enter the dark chamber, a wave of cold, dank air chills your blood. Even Essa's magical aura can't dispel the feeling of dread that sweeps over you.

"Do you feel funny, Bern?" asks Willow. Her low, husky voice has an uneasy edge to it you've never heard before. "This place is evil! I can sense it all around us!"

"I'm scared and cold! Let's get out of here!" whispers Kegan. You start to tell your brother not to worry, but Essa interrupts in her soft elven accent.

"Look at Willow's talisman!"

The healing medallion around the kender's neck has begun to glow with a pulsating purple light. Willow touches her finger to the enchanted disk, then jerks it away with a squeal of surprise.

"It's ice cold!" she exclaims.

"A powerful evil force is very near!" Essa warns.

"Perhaps we should go back," Kegan whispers.

If you decide not to risk whatever evil is lurking in this passage and go back to take the left passage, turn to **182**. If you decide to keep going ahead, turn to **28**.

196

You turn your head just in time to see Verminaard hurl a tiny object toward you. It's a miniature war hammer, like the favored weapon of mountain dwarves. In midflight, the tiny charm explodes into a dazzling spectral light that assumes the same shape as the miniature hammer but many times larger. As the spiritual hammer hurtles through the air at you, you duck, but somehow the magical weapon seems to know where you will dodge and slams into your back with the most powerful blow you've ever felt. . . .

Roll one die for damage and add two points of damage to the die roll. Then subtract the result from your hit points and turn to **17**.

197

You jab your sword under the first hobgoblin's pike, its sharp edge ripping through the guard's armor to find its mark. You pull away quickly and dodge the other hobgoblin's swing. Just then, you see a blur of motion from the corner of your eye as Willow flings her hoopak missile at the second hobgoblin's cheek just below its helmet, burying itself in the hobgoblin's yellow skin.

The hobgoblin grunts in rage and thrusts its pike at her. As soon as the creature looks away, you bring Fireborn down hard upon its right shoulder, slicing into the banded armor and forcing it to drop the pike. In an instant, Willow is on top of the wounded monster, using the butt of her hoopak as a fighting stick.

The kender moves with the precision of long practice, first cracking the hobgoblin on the bridge of its nose, then ramming the hard rod into the monster's throat when it jerks its head back. The guard gags violently and bends over to catch its breath. Willow pounces like a cat, slamming the hoopak against the base of its brain. The large creature collapses in a silent hulk next to its dead companion.

Turn to **19**.

198

Not even centuries of dust and decay can disguise the noble elven features of the skeletal corpse. His yellowed skin stretches taut across the skull, and his deathly grin seems to mock you. A cloak of rare ermine skins lies in tattered rags around the bony

184

shoulders, torn and gnawed by generations of rats. Around the dried flesh of the eerie figure's forehead, a tiara of silvery metal gleams in Essa's aura, untarnished by centuries of decay. Across the mummy's lap, there is a huge two-handed sword in a jeweled hilt.

"Kith-Kanan!" gasps Essa. The sorceress falls to her knees at the base of the throne, her beautiful elven features luminous in the magical light as she gazes in awe at the remains of what once was the greatest prince of the Qualinesti elves and the builder of Pax Tharkas!

"Then that sword in his lap must be the famous Wyrmslayer!" exclaims Willow loudly. The brash kender takes a step toward the throne, unable to contain her curiosity about the mythical weapon used by Kith-Kanan to drive the red dragons from the forest of Qualinesti.

"Stop, kender!"

Essa's gentle voice is suddenly sharp, and her green eyes flash so fiercely that even Willow hesitates. The kender turns away from the throne and stares at the sorceress, more in surprise than fear.

"The body of Lord Kith-Kanan must not be disturbed," she says with quiet authority. "This is the holiest of shrines to the elves of Qualinesti, and none but a Royal Guard of Qualinost may touch the blade called Wyrmslayer! It must remain enshrined until Kith-Kanan allows it to be drawn against the evil in this world."

Willow stares at Essa's wild eyes, realizing how serious the elven mage considers her words.

"Relax, Essa!" she says flippantly. "Talk about kender tall tales! How could Kith-Kanan give the sword to anybody in his condition? If this is really Wyrmslayer, we need to take it with us to fight Verminaard. You're the swordsman, Bern. I say you take it along!"

If you feel that this sword is much too valuable to pass up and decide to take Wyrmslayer from the Sla-Mori, turn to **77**. But if you are afraid there may be some enchantment placed on the sword of Kith-Kanan and decide it would be better to leave it undisturbed, turn to **201**.

199

Before the draconians have time to do anything, you leap across the bodies of the hobgoblins into the throne room, with Willow and Kegan right behind you. Quickly they bolt the heavy door from the inside.

"What is this? Who are you to dare such an outrage?" you hear suddenly from behind you. Turn to **116**.

From the look on Cleva's face, you know that she is not merely imagining the scene. Some horrible force did descend upon Solace—a force powerful enough to transform the lush valley of giant vallenwood trees into a smoking wasteland! But you refuse to believe it was done by creatures out of your bedtime stories.

"Where's my brother, Cleva?" you demand, trying to divert her attention from the nightmarish vision in her mind. A small glimmer of light appears in her watery eyes. "Where's Kegan?" you repeat. "What happened to him? Did these 'dragons' you saw harm him? Is he. . . ." You cannot bring yourself to say the word. Your mother's kinswoman touches your shoulder with her hand.

"Fewmaster Toede ordered the men, women, and children who survived taken to the blacksmith's shop. They're being shipped out in slave caravans to someplace called 'Pax Tharkas.' If your brother is alive, he'll be at the smith's forge."

"Toede?" Your lip curls in a sneer. "Who put that blob of blubber in charge? Where's Hederick, the High Theocrat?"

"He was taken away, Bern," Cleva says in a low voice. "Arrested."

"Arrested!" you repeat, stunned. "But he was on the Council of Highseekers! Who's in charge now?"

"Fewmaster Toede, his hobgoblin guards, and the strange, horrible creatures who call themselves 'draconians'—some sort of evil cross between men and dragons!"

"Dragons again," you mutter. "I've got to find my brother, Cleva. I'm going into Solace!"

"No!" Cleva cries, clutching your arm. "There's nothing you can do, Bern. They'll only capture you, too. Kegan will be all right. Escape now, while you've still got the chance."

If you decide there is nothing you can do to help Kegan—after all, you can't fight an entire army— turn to **144**. But if you're determined to find your younger brother, turn to **173**.

201

The intense expression on Essa's face convinces you that her warning about Wyrmslayer is much more than just a superstition. You've never met a Qualinesti elf before, but you've heard stories of their bravery and knowledge. Furthermore, this comely sorceress possesses more magical power than anyone you've ever known, and she seems ready to use it to protect the most sacred relic of her people.

"No, Willow," you tell the impatient kender, "I think we should leave that decision up to Essa. The Sla-Mori belongs to her people. We've already seen evidence of the great powers of her ancient ancestors in the hall of zombies. There are some things even a kender can scarcely understand."

Essa looks at you appreciatively, then turns to the kender. "News of the Sla-Mori and the discovery of Prince Kith-Kanan's sacred tomb will bring great honor to you among my people, Willow," she says earnestly. "You will be honored as a heroine when we return to Qualinost with our message of the Dragon Highlord's evil."

The sorceress's words seem to ease Willow's disappointment. The secretive Qualinesti elves fascinate nearly everyone in Ansalon, but Essa's promise of a welcome among them has overwhelmed the curious kender girl. She sighs, glances briefly at Kith-Kanan's corpse on the throne, and then smiles.

"On to Qualinost, then!" she exclaims. "How do we get out of here?"

"It must be the other passage leading from the intersection!" you exclaim. "It must lead to the hills below Pax Tharkas!"

"I fear I have deceived you, my friends," says Essa with an embarrassed smile. "I recognized the path my people call 'The Gate' when we stopped at the intersection. I had to find the tomb of Kith-Kanan. Now that my quest is satisfied, I can lead you to Qualinesti through the Hidden Valley below Pax Tharkas."

Essa's confession disturbs you at first, but you remember the look of awe on her lovely face as she knelt before the mummy of Kith-Kanan. You glance at Kegan and Willow and are pleased to notice their expressions of understanding.

"I understand, Essa. Sometimes I found it hard to trust you, too, partly simply because you're an elf. Perhaps this threat from Verminaard and his followers will teach us to trust each other, if we learn nothing else."

"All of you are rare among your people," says the elven mage. "We are taught in Qualinost that your races, too, cannot be trusted. Perhaps much more will come from this quest than an end to Verminaard's threat. But now come. Follow me to the gateway to the Sla-Mori!"

You have not only succeeded in escaping from Pax Tharkas, but you have also emerged from the dreaded tunnels of the Sla-Mori with your life, and your honor, intact. Reward yourself with two extra experience points next time you play this adventure.

ENDLESS QUEST® Books

From the Producers of the DUNGEONS & DRAGONS® Game

Experience all the thrills and excitement of your favorite role-playing game from TSR, Inc., in the pages of these exciting books. YOU are the hero, and only YOU can make the decisions that lead your adventure to success—or disaster!

Watch for these exciting new adventures, available SOON at better bookstores and hobby stores everywhere!

LAIR OF THE LICH
SECRET OF THE ANCIENTS